Home from the wars,
Hawkeye, Trapper, Duke and Spearchucker
meet the "Maniacs,"
bizarre rustics such as:

Dr. Doggy Moore, a lovable curmudgeon who holds office hours on the golf course, one patient per hole.

Lucinda Lively, a lissome blonde who finds Trapper—and love—in a cranberry bog.

Jocko Allcock, an orderly who makes book on the outcome of operations.

The Finch-Browns, the Hump Hill clan who are afflicted with poverty, feeblemindedness and venereal disease.

Ben Simmons, superstud lobsterman, who services the minister's wife while the Reverend is on the job.

"As hilarious as its predecessor...it might even make a funnier movie than MASH One."
—*Library Journal*

MASH GOES T
was originally pu
William Morrow

Books in the MASH Series

Mash
Mash Goes to Maine
Mash Goes to New Orleans
Mash Goes to Paris

Published by POCKET BOOKS

★M★A★S★H★
Goes to Maine

RICHARD
HOOKER

A POCKET BOOK EDITION published by
Simon & Schuster of Canada, Ltd. • Markham, Ontario, Canada
Registered User of the Trademark

MASH GOES TO MAINE

William Morrow edition published 1972

POCKET BOOK edition published January, 1973
8th printing...............November, 1974

Excerpts from this book have appeared in *Playboy* Magazine.

This POCKET BOOK edition includes every word contained in the original, higher-priced edition. It is printed from brand-new plates made from completely reset, clear, easy-to-read type. POCKET BOOK editions are published by POCKET BOOKS, a division of Simon & Schuster of Canada, Ltd., 330 Steelcase Road, Markham, Ontario L3R 2M1.
Trademarks registered in Canada and other countries.

Standard Book Number: 671-78815-9.
Library of Congress Catalog Card Number: 71-151912.

Cover art by Lawrence Ratzkin

Printed in Canada.

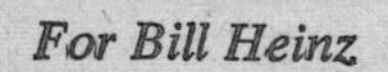

For Bill Heinz

★M★A★S★H★
Goes to Maine

1

Wendell Black, chief surgeon, USVA Hospital, Spruce Harbor, Maine, was mildly perplexed. The morning mail had brought an application from a surgeon who had trained at the College of Physicians and Surgeons and was certified by the American Board of Surgery. This surgeon was in his early forties, had prospered in private practice, inherited money, and now he wanted a job which would allow him to pursue professional interests without commercial distraction. Also, the surgeon stated, the idea of a forty-hour week fascinated him. He liked to ski, sail and play golf. Spruce Harbor, Maine, looked like the place to put it all together.

Not much in the State of Maine works like other places and this is true even in Maine's only Veterans Administration facility. Therefore Dr. Black sought the counsel of his most trusted adviser, Mr. Jocko Allcock.

To his secretary Mrs. Ames, Dr. Black said, "Would you tell Mr. Allcock I'd like to see him at his earliest convenience."

Mrs. Ames had been through this before but she always played it the same way.

"Mr. Allcock?" she asked.

"Yes, Mrs. Ames, if you please. Mr. Allcock."

"Oh, of course, Doctor. You mean Jocko."

Mr. Jocko Allcock was at the bottom of the surgical

tree on which Dr. Black, in Spruce Harbor, stood out as the highest limb. Jocko's florid, broad, blunt-nosed face sat atop six feet and two hundred and twenty pounds of muscle gradually turning to fat. He was the guy who transferred patients from the ward to the operating room, lifted or helped them onto the table, lifted them off later on and then hauled them back to the ward, or the intensive care unit, or the morgue. Jocko was also the hospital bookie and made more than his salary betting on the outcome of selected surgical procedures. Mr. Allcock had attracted the chief surgeon's attention when a patient scheduled for gastrectomy, a partial excision of the stomach, discovered that Jocko's price on him was 4 to 1, against. The patient, dismayed at the odds but wishing to participate in the action, blew his stack and the whistle when Jocko demanded payment in advance. Jocko, of course, assured the patient that he'd pay off if a payoff was possible, but he did not want to take the risk of getting stiffed because neither the government, Blue Shield or Mutual of Omaha covered this kind of arrangement.

After the furor Dr. Black and Jocko reached an accord. Dr. Black, in fact, took quite a shine to Jocko and decided that he, Jocko and maybe the Chief of Medicine were the smartest people in the Spruce Harbor VA.

So Dr. Black, who had all the surgeons he needed, was bothered by the new surgeon's application and decided to consult Jocko Allcock. Late in the morning of this sunny day in May, 1954, Dr. Black was seated behind his desk, reading the *Annals of Surgery* and surreptitiously peeking at the budding trees and the islands in Penobscot Bay. His studies and reveries were interrupted by Mr. Allcock, who said, "Hey, boss, you wanta see me?"

"Oh, yes, Mr. Allcock, come in. Cup of coffee?"

"Sure, boss. Say, you gotta butt?"

"Oh, well, er . . . sure. I think I have some here somewhere."

"Right in that top drawer, boss," Jocko told him.

"Of course. Hope you don't mind filters."

"Perfectly okay, boss. Whatcha want to see me about?"

"Read this," Dr. Black said, handing Jocko the new surgeon's application.

"What do you think, Mr. Allcock?" he asked, having allowed Jocko plenty of time to read and assimilate.

"A guy like this you can't let him git away. This guy's not old, he's got the training, he's made a living in private practice and he still wants to work. At least some. All you got now is losers or fly-by-nights gittin' in their time for the surgical boards and fixin' to leave the first time they got a grand in the bank."

"Who on the surgical staff has a grand in the bank?" asked Dr. Black.

"That christly Pierce, Hawkeye. He's beat me for a grand in the last month bettin' on his own patients. If we don't get that son of a howah outa here, I'm gonna go broke."

"Do you think I should fire him, Mr. Allcock?"

"Well, boss, he's the best man you got, but all he needs is another month here afore he's eligible for his surgical boards. He ain't gonna stay long after that so you better grab this new guy and unload Hawkeye."

"I agree, Mr. Allcock. There's just one thing. How do I fire him? I have no grounds, even though I know he spends more time on golf courses than he does here."

"Don't worry, boss. I'll take care of it."

"I'd hoped you'd say that, Mr. Allcock."

Jocko was pleased that he had been chosen to fire Dr. Pierce because he liked him and felt that Dr. Pierce, having met the training requirements specified by the American Board of Surgery, should not waste further time in the employ of the Veterans Administration. Jocko went directly to the Spruce Harbor Country Club where he knew Dr. Pierce would be hitting golf balls on the practice range.

He parked his pickup truck in the space reserved for Benny Scrubs, the pro, and approached Dr. Pierce.

"Hey, Hawkeye," Jocko said as Dr. Pierce fiddled with his grip.

"What the hell do you want?"

"Nothin'. Just wanta tell you. You're fired."

"Finestkind. I'm hitting the ball real good. Maybe I could go on the tour."

"I don't know nothin' about golf," said Jocko, who had expected a little more reaction.

Hawkeye Pierce, a tall, skinny, blond natural hooker, hit three more drives while Jocko stood and fidgeted. Then he invited Jocko to join him for lunch in the clubhouse.

"Guess I'll have a couple marts, seeing as how I'm unemployed," said Hawkeye. "How about you, Jocko?"

"Long as you're buying, I'll let it all hang out. Dr. Black said if I'd tell you about bein' fired, I could have the rest of the day off."

"I don't really care, but I suppose I should ask," said Dr. Pierce. "Why am I fired?"

"There ain't room for you in our organization, Hawkeye. I had to let you go."

"*You* had to let me go?"

"Well, yes, boy. Maybe I ain't no doctor, but I know what's best for everybody and Dr. Black respects my judgment. What's more, I been losing money on you and I been thinkin' of goin' into private practice myself."

"What are you talking about?"

"Well, boy, you go into private practice, I'll start bookin' surgery outside of the VA. I'll find out who needs operations and I'll start betting with you instead of against you and when word gets around you'll be the richest son of a howah in Maine and I'll get rich along with you. Only way I can lose is if you don't keep gittin' good results."

"Look, you stupid son of a bitch," said Dr. Pierce, "you stay the hell away from me. You got me fired. If I go into practice around here I don't need a screwball like you scaring the patients. It'll be hard enough to get started as it is, competing against the local barber surgeons."

"Boy," said Jocko, "you just don't understand, but you'll come to your senses."

Hawkeye, now on his second martini, laughed because he remembered Jocko's matchless performance at the Windsor Fair. Jocko and a fellow VA employee had erected a tent, proclaimed themselves specialists from the United States Public Health Service, and offered free rectal examinations for only fifty cents (to cover cost of the glove). Remembering that they'd made three hundred dollars before they were run off, Hawkeye said, "Maybe you're right, Jocko. We'll see."

"Whatcha gonna do now, Hawk?"

"I'm going on to a third martini to celebrate my release from the Veterans Administration. Then I shall eat a large hamburger. Then I am going to Port Waldo and visit Dr. Ralph Young and find out whether the old bastard will send me some surgery if I go into practice."

"You want me to go with you?" asked Jocko.

"It's sweet of you to offer, Jocko, but I'd like to try this on my own. I can't depend on you forever, and you've already done so much for me."

"Yeah, that's true," said Jocko, "but I'll keep an eye on you anyhow."

"My cup runneth over. Here come the hamburgers."

Later Dr. Pierce drove slowly and a mite sleepily toward Port Waldo, a village twenty miles west of Spruce Harbor and seven miles upstream from his home in Crabapple Cove. He knew the score for a young surgeon in a town like Spruce Harbor. The town had thirty thousand people and potentially served another forty to fifty thousand. The surgery was done by several general practitioner-surgeons who had little or no formal training, and what little surgery they had learned they had picked up in the school of hard knocks. The patients got the hard knocks. These doctors resented, feared and resisted the idea of a young man with five or six years of formal training coming in and doing just surgery. They'd send surgery that frightened them, and not much frightened them, to Boston or Portland. Although they wouldn't admit it to themselves, they'd rather let the patients die than give their cases to a new young surgeon. They would tell the new young surgeon that he couldn't start at the top. He had to do it like they did, develop a general practice and cull surgery from it.

Hawkeye Pierce, although a local boy, was from the outside surgical world, a world that Spruce Harbor had, so far, escaped. He knew the Spruce Harbor talent and he didn't intend to dignify these hacks by even bothering to talk to them. He also knew that there were two young specialists in internal medicine who in time would give him some work, but they weren't militant and the old gang scared them. Hawkeye believed that one doctor in Spruce Harbor, probably the best and certainly the busiest, a man named Doggy Moore, would help him, but he also figured Doggy would watch him for a year before jumping in with both feet. Hawkeye figured, finally, that he needed one busy general practitioner to feed him. Given that, plus a little from here and there, he could make a living and drive the barber surgeons into the ocean within five years.

Hawkeye decided to visit Dr. Ralph Young because Ralph always told the truth. Tall, vigorous, and happy, Dr. Young knew what he knew and what he didn't know. He had come to terms with his inadequacies. In Portland, Bangor and Boston, where he sent patients who could afford to go there for operations, he was viewed with great respect and frequently was cited as an example of what a rural practitioner should be. In Port Waldo Dr. Young, because of his honesty, escaped the total reverence in which small town and rural people frequently inundate more confident and less capable doctors. Still, he was the only one in town and he had prospered.

Hawkeye Pierce figured he'd work off the martinis before visiting Dr. Ralph Young so he drove down to Heath Point, a deserted peninsula which protrudes into Muscongus Bay and took a naked jump into the cold Atlantic. This wiped out the martinis and brought Hawkeye to the real issues. He'd had a year of internship, three years of surgical residency, two years of army surgery, and a year of surgery in VA. How many years? Seven out of medical school. Not broke, but close to it. A wife, Mary, and three kids: Billy, age six, Stephen, age five, and nine-month-old Karen. And he was eligible for the surgical boards, so he would make out in private practice if he were patient. But, damn it, he felt unfulfilled. Surgery was jumping in the outside world. He had come back from Korea, sick of the army and cities and wanting to stay home in Maine. Now, a year later, he wondered if he belonged in Crabapple Cove and Spruce Harbor. He wondered if he should give himself a chance in the big time.

Uncertain of what he wanted, he called on Dr. Ralph Young, who had just finished office hours and was expecting Hawkeye.

"Hi, Hawk," he said, "I've been waiting for you. Jocko called. I hear you're going into private practice and want all my surgery."

"Yeah, I guesso. That christless Jocko seems to want to be my business manager."

"Okay, Hawkeye," said Dr. Young, "I'll lay it on the line. You're still only—what? Thirty-one?"

"Around there."

"You have the general surgical training. If you go into practice I'll send you everything I can dig up. But, if you'll listen to your old twenty-dollar obstetrician, you'll get the hell out of here. This area is going to open up. We'll have trained surgeons in Spruce Harbor within five years. You'll be competing with your own kind. Get a couple of years of training in thoracic surgery under your belt and nobody can touch you. You can come back here and be the big man in chest cutting. If you do that, you'll automatically get your share of the general surgery."

"I've been thinking about the same way, Ralph," said Dr. Pierce. "But, Jesus, I got very little dough. At the age of thirty-one, with three kids, I don't know if Mary will hold still for another couple years of residency and debt."

"I waited two years for Big Benjy Pierce to pay twenty bucks for you."

"Yeah, you old bastard, and you were lucky to get it. I'll let you know what I decide."

"I'll see you, Hawk," said Dr. Young, who laughed

after Hawkeye left and said to himself, "That boy heard me."

Hawkeye mounted the big brown '52 Chrysler he had bought secondhand after getting out of Korea, and drove slowly toward Crabapple Cove and the little house on the edge of the Cove where he, Mary, Bill, Steve and Karen were living, just across a tidal inlet from his father's farm. The kids, he knew, would be at the farm and Mary, adding to the family wealth by teaching school, would be at a convention in Bangor. He would be all alone. He would have a drink and take another swim. It was a happy prospect because he really needed to think.

Dr. Pierce turned down Pierce Road. Nobody but Pierces had ever lived in this part of Crabapple Cove and he was more vividly aware of his surroundings than he had been for months. He loved the fields and the pines and firs and spruce along the shore and the high tide and the low tide and he didn't ever want to leave them. From the top of the hill, he saw Big Benjy Pierce's lobster boat moored in the channel. He saw his kids and his nephews and nieces playing in his father's barnyard across the tidal inlet from his own little house, where a new robin's-egg-blue Pontiac convertible was parked in the driveway.

"Now who the hell is that?" he asked himself. "Holy old baldheaded Jesus," he exclaimed, after a moment of logical thought and a look at the Massachusetts plates. "It's the Trapper. Trapper John. It has to be because he always talked about blue Pontiac convertibles."

Trapper was his buddy from the 4077th MASH in Korea where Hawkeye had spent eighteen months as a surgeon during the Police Action. He'd been expecting Trapper. Trapper had stayed behind and been sent to Okinawa after the truce. When he and Duke Forrest had left their tent, The Swamp, fifteen months back, Trapper John had been half in the bag, weeping, but now he was out of the army and in Crabapple Cove.

Hawkeye had known Trapper for a year in Korea, but people in Korea and people at home are not necessarily the same. Hawk approached the meeting with a mixture of joy and doubt. He pulled in beside the blue convertible, went in the back door, walked through the kitchen. From there he saw Trapper, with a beer, sitting on the flimsy front porch, beneath which three feet of salt water flowed at high tide. Trapper was drowsily taking in the scene, the cove, the lobster boats and Big Benjy Pierce's wharf opposite Hawkeye's house.

Trapper didn't hear him coming so Hawk had a chance to appraise his visitor. The grubby, unshaven, long-haired army surgeon was a new man, at least on the surface. Still thin, he was dressed tastefully and expensively and Hawkeye, perhaps for the first time, really believed that Trapper John McIntyre was what he was supposed to be, a bright, young, capable thoracic and cardiovascular surgeon. Why, he wondered, did seeing Trapper dressed up make a difference? Well, it didn't really, but Hawkeye had feared that the civilian Trapper would be exactly like the military Trapper.

Hawk opened the porch door and said, "Hi, Trapper. Where you been? I figured you for a month ago."

"I had to spend a month in bed to catch up. Now I'm all caught up so I figured I'd come and get you off the clam flats."

"What you got in mind?"

"Maxie Neville wants me to come to Saint Lombard's in New York and help him do the heart surgery. You're going to get a year of thoracic surgical residency at some VA joint in Jersey where Maxie is the consultant and then you're going to come to work for me and Maxie."

"Jeez, Trapper, you don't mean it. You and me and Maxie Neville?"

"Screw you. Stay here if you want to."

"I want to, but I'll bite for two years of your deal. Enough to get the thoracic boards. Then I'm coming right back here. Now that we've settled so much so simply, let's discuss important things."

2

Two months later, in July, Dr. and Mrs. Pierce, with Billy, Steve and Karen, left Crabapple Cove for the big VA Hospital in New Jersey. Someone at the hospital had found them "a nice two-bedroom apartment in a nice apartment development." The kind of place where even if a guy comes home sober he's lucky to figure out where he lives.

The Big VA Hospital turned out to be in a deadfall which the natives of the place called East Orange. This was located in North Jersey, which is just north of a place called South Jersey.

Hawkeye's first day on his new job was devoted to filling out various forms and questionnaires. A secretary assigned to assist him was happy to see the last of him. He had bought a second car, a '41 Chevy, from a kid brother who was in jail. On the appropriate form he described the vehicle as a '41 Corvette.

The secretary had never heard of a '41 Corvette but accepted the explanation that it was the only one of its kind. She was less happy when Hawkeye asked, "Hey, who's the Chief Surgeon in this oversized cement mausoleum? Dr. Hyde?"

"I don't know any Dr. Hyde," she told him.

"Ma'am, if I knew anything would I be here? I gather they got some nice pig farms in Secaucus. Is that anywhere around here?"

"I'm afraid I don't know."

"You ever been to Newark?" Hawk asked.

"Of course."

"You ever been to Maine?"

"No, sir, I haven't."

"What a pity," observed Hawkeye.

Hawkeye, who had been his own boss in Korea and Spruce Harbor VA, had accepted responsibility beyond his years. He was not in the habit of taking much guff from anybody, particularly the likes of Jimmy Gargan, the Chief of Thoracic Surgery at East Orange VA. Jimmy, a black Irishman about half the size of big blond Hawkeye Pierce, was a perfectionist who criticized everything Hawk did, right down to how he got into an operating-room gown.

After four days in the OR, Hawkeye decided to kill Jimmy Gargan. The only thing he couldn't decide was how to go about it. After two weeks, Gargan let Hawkeye do an easy right upper lobectomy—he took out the upper third of the right lung—and harassed him from start to finish.

By this time Hawkeye had rejected homicide and decided that although Gargan wasn't his type he was an all-pro chest cutter. He decided to swallow his pride.

After Hawkeye's first lobectomy, Gargan said over coffee, "You don't like me, do you, Pierce?"

"Not particularly."

"Few people do. In fact I drive half my residents away within three months. How long do you think you'll last?"

"The whole year. As far as I'm concerned you're a little bog-Irish mammy-jammer. But I've learned more from you in two weeks than I ever learned anywhere else in six months. You'll have to fire me before I'll leave."

"I don't think I will. I've been trying to get a rise out of you. I keep getting all kinds of big blond prima donnas that the Maxie Nevilles and their kind send in here. They can't take the kind of crap I deal out."

"You come on like a son of a bitch but you seem to be a pro. I came here to learn how to jerk out lungs, so I'll take anything you can dish out as long as I figure I'm gaining on something."

"You've got me on the defensive, now. No one's done that in quite a while. But I don't like being called an S.O.B."

"Oh, Christ," Hawkeye said. "Your trouble is that you obviously don't think there's anything important in the world besides hearts and lungs, so I just can't identify with you. I'll pick your brain and take your shit for a year and go on my way and you'll still be here when I'm back in Maine doing what you're doing and living like a human being in the bargain."

"Do I read you right?" Gargan asked. "Do you really feel superior to anyone who is happy to live and is interested in doing a good job in northern New Jersey?"

"In a way," said Hawkeye. "Let's just say I feel luckier. For Chrissake, that middle-income housing development someone's stuck me into is an insult. The whole joint smells like someone boiled a goat, hair and all. Any tarpaper shack with an outdoor john in Maine would be better."

Jimmy Gargan sipped his coffee and reflected a moment before saying, "By the way, the Chief Surgeon asked me to mention that he doesn't like to be called 'Dad.' "

"Who in hell is the Chief Surgeon? I thought you were."

"Dr. Rizzo is the Chief Surgeon, as you certainly must know."

"Which fat guinea is he?" asked Hawkeye.

"I don't think you really mean everything you say," Jimmy Gargan said. "But either way, I have an idea we'll get along."

Jimmy Gargan and Hawkeye Pierce avoided friendship but achieved mutual respect. Maxie Neville, who visited East Orange as a consultant every two weeks, was pleased with Hawkeye and relieved that Trapper John's recommendation was based on more than friendship.

Thoracic surgery in 1954 and 1955 when Hawkeye was in East Orange was still a young specialty. A lung was removed successfully for the first time in 1933 by Evarts Graham and J. J. Singer. A handful of young men went into thoracic surgery after that. By 1955 these men were in their fifties and, although not old, they were patriarchs of a specialty which did not establish a certifying board of its own until 1948. The patriarchs, of whom Maxie Neville was one, examined new candidates for the club with extreme care and ran their specialty with the autocracy of Cosa Nostra chieftains.

Maxie Neville had the build and the walk of a middle-weight fighter, which he had been. He had thick curly gray hair and chiseled features which looked weather beaten. Maxie attributed his appearance to a weekly ferry ride to the Public Health Service Hospital on Staten Island. Maxie had a pair of half-glasses which, if he wore them at all, he peered over more often than through. His blue eyes were always moving and missed very little, particularly females between the ages of twenty and fifty. Jimmy Cagney could have played Maxie Neville in the movies but the chances are that Maxie, himself, could have done it better and he wouldn't have needed a stunt man to do the surgery.

Maxie reduced the selection of new club members to a very simple formula. First, they had to come with strong recommendations from someone he knew and respected. In Hawkeye's case, he knew Trapper John, the boy wonder of Boston, and Trapper's old boss, Billy Morrow. Step number two was to give the candidate a year on one of the farm clubs, like East Orange VA. If the candidate survived eight months of that year, Maxie seriously considered him for a year on his service at Saint Lombard's in New York. This year, in addition to hospital duties, involved participation in Maxie's private practice, which was a high-class practice in every respect, including price. Many patients came to Maxie from Europe, South America and from every state in the union. Maxie did not want helpers who could not adjust to his clientele.

So, at the eight-month point, Maxie took a personal look. This was known as Maxie's final exam and the stories about it varied. Those who failed maintained that he accepted or rejected people purely on whim without consideration of ability, hard work or anything else that should be meaningful. Maxie started his in-depth investigation of Hawkeye Pierce by questioning Jimmy Gargan.

"How about this clamdigger from Maine? Do you like him?"

"I don't dislike him. Maybe I'd like him if he liked me. All I can say is he's the best man I've had here. He's all business. He's teachable. The patients all like him. They like him better than me. I can talk to a patient and tell him he needs surgery and he'll say no. Pierce can go in half an hour later and have the guy begging for an operation."

"Why doesn't he like you?" asked Dr. Neville.

"This guy really hates cities. I think he really believes he is a member of a master race because he grew up in the country. Hell, I've hardly ever even seen a cow and I like cities. I've never been out of one. I think Pierce reacts to me in the same way he reacts to cities."

Maxie Neville, who'd grown up on a ranch in Wyoming, chuckled. "Can you spare Pierce for a while?" he asked. "I think I'll take him to lunch."

An hour later Hawkeye Pierce, having completed the finger fracture of a mitral valve with Dr. Neville looking over his shoulder, was told by Dr. Gargan that the time had come. Lunch with Maxie. The final exam.

"Meet him in the parking lot at twelve thirty. Good luck."

"You mean that, Jimbo?"

"I wish you wouldn't call me Jimbo. Yes, I mean it, Pierce."

"Hey, Jim," said Hawkeye. "Just for the record. If I blow this exam, no hard feelings. I know what you told Maxie."

"How do you know?"

"I know because I know that, although you've led a disadvantaged life, you are solid to the core. In fact, I'm quite fond of you. If you'd learn to speak English, instead of the local dialect, I might even take you to my heart."

"Go!" roared the small thoracic surgeon.

Dr. Pierce was apprehensive as he approached the parking lot. He had invested almost a year in this adventure and it would be wasted if Maxie didn't give him the next year at Saint Lombard's. He would have to go home, no richer, with some chest training but not enough to qualify for the thoracic boards. Trapper John was confident Hawkeye would pass but had not leaned on Maxie because Maxie always called the final shot. Nor had Trapper coached Hawkeye. He had faith in Hawk's managerial instinct. Be loose, Hawkeye told himself as he approached Dr. Maxie Neville's Cadillac convertible.

"You drive," Dr. Neville ordered. "I have to go to the hospital in Passaic. Couple people over there I want you to meet."

"Okay."

"What would you like to talk about?" asked Dr. Neville. "Thoracic surgery or fucking?"

"Which are you best at?"

"Pull up in the middle of the next block in front of that beer joint. Double park if you have to."

Hawkeye parked and followed Maxie into the small dark beer parlor where the great surgeon ordered two beers and two sausages which were floating in a foul liquid in a big grimy jug. Maxie looked at Hawkeye and said, "I'm from Wyoming. I don't know why I am here. I understand you're going back to Maine."

"Uh-huh."

"Are you leaving soon or are you willing to spend a year with me at Saint Lombard's?"

"I shouldn't wonder," agreed Hawkeye.

"You shouldn't wonder what?"

"I'd like to spend a year at Saint Lombard's and I

shouldn't wonder but what I could use another beer, as long as you're buyin'."

"Make it fast," said Maxie, "and drive back to the hospital. The examination is over."

3

Dr. and Mrs. Pierce decided that a year in New York for Mary and the kids, on top of a year in East Orange, would be cruel and inhuman torture. Hawkeye managed to get off the month of June and they all returned to Crabapple Cove. A whole beautiful month in the State of Maine. Leisure, fresh air, saltwater, clams, lobsters, golf, no responsibility, even a little money in their pockets, because Daddy had passed the general surgical boards and the VA had increased his salary to eleven grand a year.

At the end of June, Hawkeye Pierce, alone and unhappy at the thought of leaving his family, departed for New York City in the '41 Corvette to spend a year with Dr. Maxwell Neville and Dr. John Francis Xavier McIntyre at Saint Lombard's Hospital. "I must be out of my jeezly skull," Hawkeye (who talked to cars) said to the Corvette as he aimed it down the Maine turnpike. A few weeks later, Hawkeye was sure he was out of his mind. His problem, though, was deciding whether he liked it or not.

Dr. Pierce found himself in surgical excitement and

competition and challenge which relatively few, in any profession, experience. Looking back years later, he was amused by it, but in 1955 he was excited. Heart surgery, the thoracic surgeon's new frontier, was a thrilling adventure.

When he was out of it and time had passed, Hawkeye named the world he'd left the Cardia Nostra. It worked very much like Cosa Nostra. It all started back in '49 when Big Billy in Boston and Big Charley in Philly both operated on a diseased nonfunctioning valve, the mitral, which separates the left atrium of the heart from the left ventricle. They did these operations and got away with them (which means a live, rehabilitated patient) on the same day. Each claimed priority and fame with the passion and tenacity of a pair of hoods who might have, firing simultaneously, shot J. Edgar Hoover. The Cardia Nostra was divided into families, each headed by a patriarch, or don, like Big Billy in Boston, Big Maxie in New York, Big Charley in Philly and Big Mike in Houston. Each don had lieutenants and varying numbers of soldiers (residents). In New York, Big Maxie's lieutenant was Trapper John. Hawkeye Pierce, a soldier, was soon half-soldier half-lieutenant because of his good connections.

Until the late forties, the chest was a tough place in which to work for many physiological reasons. The original thoracic surgeons, like most adventurers and pioneers, were smart, egotistical and piratical. Like Columbus, Leif Ericson, Jacques Cartier, they wanted to get somewhere first. Maxie Neville wanted to be the first man to resect the aortic arch, the big artery just north of the heart where blood starts its journey to every nook and cranny of the body. He never made it, nor did several patients, even though Hawkeye Pierce broke all speed records transporting calves' aortas, with which Maxie hoped to replace human aortas, from a kosher butcher shop on the Lower East Side to Saint Lombard's Hospital.

"I ain't a surgeon," Hawk complained to Trapper John one day. "I'm just a driver. I drive calves' aortas to beat hell. That don't learn me no surgery."

"If you don't like driving calves' aortas," counseled Trapper John, "why don't you go home and milk your old man's cow?"

The whole clue to successful surgery inside the heart is a pump and oxygenator which will take the place of the heart and lungs long enough for the surgeon to do his bit. In 1955 all the dons had their lieutenants and soldiers working on such rigs and many industrial types were working with the various families and everyone had a slightly different pump oxygenator. Everyone wanted to come up with the best and the number of dogs knocked off in this experimental race could equal the number of human lives saved, prolonged or made easier. Maxie told one of his soldiers, at a chest club in Brooklyn, to make a gas-permeable membrane which could supply oxygen to blood circulated through it. The soldier complied but, four months later, Maxie looked at the membrane oxygenator and said: "Orville, you're grounded. That won't fly."

In this instance, Orville, never a happy soldier, blew his bankroll on cab fare to the Jersey side of the George Washington Bridge and hitchhiked to Cleveland with the membrane oxygenator cradled like a baby in his lap. In Cleveland the paterfamilias of the Cardia Nostra was Big Amos, a don somewhat younger than Big Maxie. Big Amos saw hope for Orville's membrane oxygenator and soon Orville was a lieutenant in the organization of Big Amos, who derived great pleasure out of one-upping Big Maxie. This engendered a certain amount of ill feeling and Orville was prohibited from taking the Thoracic Surgical

Boards for ten years, but otherwise he prospered and is now the don of a small family of his own in upstate New York.

In 1947 the heart was surgically unapproachable. Twenty years later hearts could be transplanted with technical, if not immunological, success. Dr. Hawkeye Pierce, caught in the excitement of it all, came to enjoy it, despite separation from his family and intense dislike for New York City. Dr. Maxwell Neville, who watched all his soldiers closely, found that Pierce, while clearly lacking Trapper John's superintelligence, was a competent, efficient, reflective surgeon who could, if the situation called for it, abandon his Maine accent and gain the confidence of Maxie's diverse and very sick clientele. This made life easier for Maxie and this is what good soldiers are for.

Three or four times a month Hawkeye would be sent off by plane or car to spy on Big Jimmy in Washington, Big George in Pittsburgh, or Big Charley in Philly. He would be met by a soldier from one of these families, have a drink or even dinner with the don himself and spend a day in his operating room and laboratory. This was not called spying. It was called an exchange of ideas. Big Charley in Philly was the most flamboyant of the dons. Big Charley had more soldiers than any other don and many of them were Filipinos. America, then, was the hotbed of cardiac surgery, and young surgeons from all over the world enlisted in the Cardia Nostra. In Hawkeye's opinion, every Filipino who wasn't a mess boy in the navy was a soldier in the army of Big Charley, who at that time worked in a very old hospital with very small operating rooms.

Big Maxie Neville was extremely anxious to exchange ideas with Big Charley, so Hawkeye visited Philly quite often.

"Let me know about that pump of his. Will it do

everything he says, or is he just bullshitting everybody?" said Maxie.

After four trips to Philly, Big Charley addressed Dr. Pierce as Hawkeye and invited him to scrub in on the resection of a left ventricular aneurysm, a partial blowout of the main chamber of the heart. That made it four surgeons, three scrub nurses, two circulating nurses, Big Charley's pump-oxygenator which was the biggest in the Cardia Nostra and the eight Filipino soldiers who made it run.

Driving back to New York that night Hawkeye realized that he'd probably never get smart enough to understand all the intricate physiology, hydraulic engineering and physics involved in this game. He stopped for a drink in a little town off the Jersey Turnpike. He sat at the bar and chuckled over a double Scotch. Eight. Count 'em. Eight Filipinos to run the jeezly pump.

Next day, during a pneumonectomy, removal of a lung, Maxie asked, "Well, tell me. Has Charley got anything?"

"Max," said Hawkeye, "as far as I can tell all he has is some kind of maze with Filipinos crawling around in it. I was right there assisting him and I couldn't tell whether it was an operation or a Huk insurrection."

And so it came to pass that, after six months in the Cardia Nostra, Dr. Benjamin Franklin Pierce of Crabapple Cove, Maine, was considered to have lieutenant potential. The paths open to him included permanent association with Big Maxie, association with Big Julius in Dallas, or taking over Big Maxie's already established cardiac surgical concession at a large hospital in North Jersey.

Big Maxie and Trapper John McIntyre were leaning

on Hawkeye to make a decision, but Hawkeye was reluctant. "I'll think about it," he said.

"What's to think about?" asked Trapper as the three of them sipped Scotch in Maxie's office one evening, after the last patient had left.

"Well," said Hawk, "I sure as hell ain't going to Texas, and I'm kind of scared to stay around here."

"Why?" asked Maxie.

"Because it says in the *Farmer's Almanac* that the Lord's going to give the world an enema before the year 2000 and He's going to stick the nozzle either here or in Calcutta. I got my family to think of. My insurance doesn't cover tidal waves."

Trapper John was very annoyed with his old buddy, but Maxie Neville, from Wyoming, said, "Don't worry about it, Hawk. Anything you decide is okay. If you want to go home after this year, do it. I'll see you through the Thoracic Boards. A good chest surgeon won't do any harm in Spruce Harbor, Maine."

Hawkeye, immediately and forever, was grateful for these words from Maxie Neville. Maxie was willing to push Hawkeye in the big league, but, because Maxie was a country boy, he knew that Hawkeye didn't belong in New York, or Dallas, or North Jersey. Trapper John, then, didn't understand because he was from Boston.

As though on cue, there was loud conversation in the secretary's office, just as Max Neville blessed Hawkeye's return to Spruce Harbor.

"This here Hawkeye Pierce's office?" they heard.

"This is Dr. Maxwell Neville's office. Dr. Pierce is his resident," said Bette, the secretary.

"Hawkeye around?"

Dr. Neville heard this, got up, walked to the secretary's office and saw two visitors who could only have come from Spruce Harbor, Maine: Jocko Allcock and

Wooden Leg Wilcox, the One-Legged Bandit of Ocean Street, Spruce Harbor's leading wholesale fish dealer. Wooden Leg had been a college classmate and fraternity brother of Hawkeye's.

Confronted by Maxie Neville, Jocko and Wooden Leg suddenly felt conspicuous and ill at ease, but Maxie smiled and said, "If you guys are looking for Hawkeye, come on back and have a drink."

The guests were subdued only briefly. Given a Scotch and soda, Wooden Leg said. "Jesus Christ, ain't this something? Go to a doctor's office and get a drink. I always knew medicine was more advanced in the city."

"You betcher ass, boy," agreed Mr. Allcock.

"Why the hell are you guys in New York?" asked Hawkeye.

"Mostly to see you wasn't backslidin'," Jocko answered. "We talked to Mary and she said you was thinkin' of stayin' down heah and not comin' home."

"That and Jocko wants to change his luck," said Wooden Leg. "I figured I'd drop him off in Greenwich Village and go down and look around the Fulton Fish Market."

Maxie Neville scribbled a Village address on a prescription blank and handed it to Jocko. "Go here," he said. "Ask for Alice. Say Max sent you."

"Jesus, he's a pimp, too," Wooden Leg whispered loudly to Hawkeye.

"Max," said Hawkeye, "don't do too much too quick for these grunts. While appreciating your help, they'll tend to misinterpret your sure touch with urban refinements."

Max smiled and said, "Don't worry. I get no patients from Spruce Harbor. What do you guys have in mind for Hawkeye?"

"We're gonna manage Hawkeye," replied Jocko.

"The whole thing depends on him bein' the best around. We know you're okay. Dr. Neville, because we looked you up. Now what we gotta know is whether Hawkeye is any good in the chest. If he ain't, me and Wooden Leg gonna take a christly bath. If he is, we can clean up bettin' with him 'cuz the word in Maine is all chest surgical patients croak, and there ain't no problem gitten' people to bet against them."

"I don't really understand your program," said Dr. Neville, "but I think if you manage it judiciously you'll achieve a measure of success."

"Finestkind," said Wooden Leg.

"Ayuh," agreed Jocko.

"Just what is your plan?" asked Hawkeye. "I'd like to be among the first to know."

"Simplest thing in the world," explained Jocko. "We're gonna book bets on all major surgery done in Spruce Harbor, by you or anybody else. But the odds we're gonna offer on your patients are gonna be more in favor of the patient than if they go to Ramsey Coffin or old Wiley Morgan. For example, say somebody has to have their gallbladder out. If they go to Coffin or Morgan we're gonna say there's one chance in ten, or maybe twenty, dependin' on his age and general condition, the guy ain't goin' to walk out of the hospital. If they go to you, we're gonna say there's one chance in two hundred, or thereabouts, that he won't make it. We gotta make money because you won't lose no routine surgery and Ramsey and Wiley are as bad as the odds we'll be givin' on them. Furthermore, when the word gets around, everybody'll be comin' to you anyhow and by that time our business oughta be well established."

"Oh, my sweet Jesus," moaned Hawkeye.

"It certainly is an interesting approach," said Dr.

Maxwell Neville, "but who are you going to get to bet on this sort of thing?"

"The jeezly guineas," Wooden Leg told him. "They'll bet on anything. They'll get us started and then the shitkickers will jump on."

"What is a shitkicker?" asked Dr. Neville.

"Jesus, Max, didn't you ever play baseball in a cow pasture where something else looks like second base?"

"I understand," said Dr. Neville.

Jocko, Maxie, Trapper and Wooden Leg continued the discussion while Hawkeye sat and thought. Really, nothing unethical about the arrangement. Certainly not as unethical as the lousy surgery perpetrated by Ramsey Coffin and Wiley Morgan. What's more, it could work. There were, perhaps, a thousand Italians in Spruce Harbor, all fishermen or related to fishermen, and Wooden Leg Wilcox had them all in his pocket. During working hours, Mr. Wilcox began nearly all sentences with, "Look, you fucking guinea," and the Italian population responded unfailingly with the endearing rejoinder, "Look, you fuckin' One-Legged Bandit." Regardless of the words, the guineas and Wooden Leg had great mutual respect. Leg had inherited the business from his father and had proved himself just as honest.

Hawkeye remembered asking a fisherman, "How come you guys take so much shit from Wooden Leg?"

"Whadda yuh mean, Hawk?"

"Well, all this guinea stuff."

"Hawk," said the fisherman, "it ain't what a man calls you. It's how he uses you, and Wooden Leg uses everybody good. Like last week Dominic come in with a trip of fish. He knew Leg was all bought up so he tries to sell it to them other places. They couldn't touch it and Leg knew they couldn't. He's watchin' Dominic's boat and he says, 'Where's that fuckin' Dominic? Don't he know I gotta have fish?' So I call Dominic on that bullhorn Leg has and Dominic comes in and Leg says, 'I gotta have fish and I'll give you a nickel a pound and not a cent more, you fuckin' guinea thief.' So Leg gives Dominic two hundred dollars and tells Shine to go dump the fish. 'Course it works the other way, too. When the market's good, Leg gets our fish and all the other guys get is what Leg don't need, but it's Wooden Leg takes care of us, no matter what."

"Well, really, it's just good business on his part, isn't it?"

"Look, Hawkeye," said the fisherman. "I know your father and I know you, but don't nobody come down to this here waterfront and badmouth Wooden Leg Wilcox. I don't care who."

"Hey, Hawkeye," said Jocko Allcock, interrupting Dr. Pierce's peaceful recollection of Wooden Leg and the Italian fishermen. "We got it worked out how to get you off to a fast start. You gotta apply for your privileges at Spruce Harbor General right off because about two months afore you start practice you're gonna make a guest appearance and take out Pasquale's left lung."

"I am? Who the hell is Pasquale?"

"Pasquale Merlino. He's sixty-two years old. He's got bronchiectasis in his whole left lung. His right lung is good. He don't smoke no more. He's got a normal electrocardiogram. I had Dr. Black see him and he says he's a good risk but them jerks has told him an operation would kill him."

"So?"

"Well," said Jocko, "me and Wooden Leg and your old man, Big Benjy, has all talked to Pasquale and Pasquale says he'll let you try to take his lung out. He ain't no good, coughin' up that mess all the time, so he figures he ain't got nothin' to lose."

"Where do you guys come in?"

"We're gonna have ten grand with him and we can get three to one, easy, from the guineas," said Wooden Leg. "They want him to get well, but they're sure he can't make it and they won't turn down a bargain."

"So you guys will make thirty grand and I'm lucky if I get paid?"

"We'll pay the surgeon's fee and this'll give us what we need to git rollin'," said Jocko. "If you pull this one off we got two other chest cases lined up for you. Also three bad-risk gallbladders the quacks won't touch."

"Hawkeye," said Maxie Neville, "I think you'd better stay here."

"No," Hawkeye said reflectively, "I guess I'll give it a go. I'll take Trapper along to operate on Pasquale. Maybe we can do the other chest cases before I actually start practice. You'll give me a few half-weeks off, won't you?"

"Far be it from me to stop surgical progress," said Maxie.

4

On a Wednesday in April of 1956, Hawkeye Pierce and Trapper John McIntyre left Saint Lombard's Hospital and drove to Spruce Harbor, Maine, where on Friday they removed Pasquale Merlino's left lung.

This, the first pneumonectomy ever done at Spruce Harbor General, made everyone nervous except the surgeons and the anesthesiologist, Dr. Ezekiel Bradbury (Me Lay) Marston. Early in his career, as a result of saying "Me Lay, you lay?" to so many young damsels, Dr. Marston had become exhausted. He chose, therefore, a sedentary occupation.

"It's a pleasure to work with you guys," Me Lay declared in the doctors' dressing room after the operation. "I'm tired of Ramsey Coffin and Wiley Morgan."

"What's with them?" asked Hawkeye.

"This Coffin is our age. He's had very little surgical training but he talks a big game. He has superficial technical facility and the large personality. Broads of all ages take one look at him and want to lie down. They don't care if he sticks a scalpel or anything else into them."

"And Wiley?"

"Until ten years ago he was okay because he was ahead of anyone else doing surgery around here. Now he's too old and he should quit, but he's not about to. He's lost sight of reality and the public suffers. Fortunately, they suffer happily because they don't know any better. They think an old guy who trained himself is far superior to a young guy out of a good surgical residency program."

"Who's Doggy Moore use for surgery?"

"He uses both these guys for stuff he thinks they can do. He does a little himself. The rest he sends to Bangor and Portland."

"You think Doggy will use me?"

"Sooner or later," said Me Lay. "Doggy takes nobody's word for anything. He waits and watches. When he finally makes up his mind, there'll need to be three of you because he sees more patients and finds more surgery than anybody else."

"Wasn't Doggy Chipmunk Moore's father? asked Hawkeye.

"Sort of," said Me Lay.

Both Me Lay and Hawkeye were silent for a moment. Then Trapper John asked: "Who was Chipmunk Moore?"

"I'm not sure," said Hawkeye, "but he was something else."

"That," Trapper complained, "is about as clear an answer as anyone in Maine ever gives me."

"What about the rest of the talent around here?" Hawkeye asked Me Lay. "Anybody new besides this Coffin character?"

"The rest are okay. We have two good internists and most of the general practitioners are competent. Probably the biggest problem is Goofus MacDuff. Actually he's more pest than problem. Somebody decided we had to have a Medical Director and the job description calls for chicken shit. Goofus doesn't know whether Christ was crucified or went down with the *Titanic* so he won the job by acclamation."

"Goofus!" exclaimed Hawkeye. "Is he that tall, skinny, redheaded clown who was a couple years ahead of us at Androscoggin? Looked like a toothbrush with hair?"

"He's the one, but don't worry. Just laugh at him. Don't let him bother you."

"Guys like that bother me," said Hawk, "if they have titles. I've heard about a Limey practicing over in Eagle Head. What's the word on him?"

"That's Tony Holcombe," said Me Lay. "He's doing a damn good job. He flew a Spitfire in the Battle of Britain and that background didn't equip him for the

National Health Service so he came over here. You'll like him. Let's go to the coffee shop."

Jocko Allcock and Wooden Leg Wilcox were there, anxiously awaiting news of the operation. "You fix Pasquale?" Jocko asked as the surgeons entered.

"Did we have a choice?"

"Sure. You could cool him and take your chances with the guineas."

"Hell, they're all betting against," complained Trapper.

"They are of two minds but they'd rather lose their dough than Pasquale."

Dr. Goofus MacDuff joined them and said, "Nice to have you fellows, but gee, Pasquale's been getting along okay. I'm not so sure he needed to have the lung out."

"If I had any early doubt, you've just removed it, Goofus," Hawkeye told him.

"I don't know," said Goofus. "Do you think we're ready for this kind of surgery here?"

"Hey, you. I don't like you," said Trapper, who fixed Goofus with a malignant stare.

Dr. MacDuff suddenly remembered he had business elsewhere.

The surgeons watched Pasquale over the weekend and, satisfied with his progress, returned to New York on Monday. They returned for two more guest appearances before July when, nine years after his graduation from medical school, the time finally came for Hawkeye Pierce to enter private practice. Dr. Pierce entered with more of a bang than most surgeons enjoy. Jocko had lined up the three poor-risk gallbladders and Hawkeye did all three of them his first week. All got along well, mostly because they weren't really poor-risk patients. They were just fat. Ralph Young in Port Waldo had been saving a few hernias and a carcinoma of the rectum. After three weeks in practice, Dr. Tony Holcombe approached Dr. Pierce and said: "Hello, Hawkeye. I guess you and I should have a talk."

"Finestkind," said Hawkeye.

"Don't drown me in the local jargon," said Tony, "particularly when I'm about to make you my surgeon."

"I'd like to be your surgeon."

"I'm just a bloody general practitioner," Tony Holcombe said, "but I won't have my patients anywhere near those two quacks who've been doing the surgery here."

Tony and Hawkeye, although opposites in many ways, became friends. In the operating room Tony was a hopelessly inept assistant but his clinical knowledge and judgment were of the highest caliber. Although Tony was more culturally advanced than Hawkeye they found many common, extramedical interests. For Hawkeye, Tony filled the void created by the loss of Trapper John and Maxie Neville and the other urban hotshots.

Throughout Hawkeye's first months in practice he was being watched closely by Doggy Moore, Spruce Harbor's busiest and most versatile doctor. Nothing, in or out of medicine, had happened in Spruce Harbor for more than thirty years that Doggy Moore didn't know about, so he knew about the betting on Hawkeye's patients and he knew that Jocko Allcock, Wooden Leg and Ralph Young were preparing Hawkeye for stardom. Still, Doggy wanted to wait and see for himself.

While Doggy was sniffing at Hawkeye, Hawkeye was sniffing at Doggy, and the more he sniffed the more fascinated he became. Doggy, in 1956, was about sixty-three years old, a tall, gray-haired, big-boned, sometimes loud-voiced, sometimes mumbling giant of a man who'd played three sports at Androscoggin College and who, twice, had been the Maine Amateur Golf Champion. He was called Doggy because in his station wagon, or pickup truck, whichever he chose to drive, there were always two Chesapeake Bay retrievers. Doggy had them along partly to chase rabbits, partly for company and partly to guard the golf clubs, fishing poles, shotgun and rifle which he always carried with him.

Doggy took care of more sick people than anyone else. He played as much golf as anyone else. He shot as many rabbits and birds as anyone else. He caught more fish and shot more deer than anyone else.

In Spruce Harbor the prevailing opinion was that Doggy Moore might be able to walk on water. Other doctors had patients only because no one, not even Doggy Moore, could take care of everybody. Up until the age of fourteen, the citizens of Spruce Harbor addressed Dr. Moore as Dr. Doggy. Reaching puberty, they addressed him as Doggy. In drugstores, garages, grocery stores, wherever he went, it was "Hi, Doggy. How they goin', Doggy?" He could have made a career of just walking through town looking at pictures of kids he'd delivered. He was called "Dr. Moore" only on the hospital page system. Smyrna Boggs, the switchboard operator, would say, "Dr. Moore, telephone please," but if he didn't answer immediately and Smyrna thought it might be important, she'd yell, "Doggy, will you please answer the phone?"

Although some of the competition had evening and Saturday office hours (a horrible habit which still exists in some rural areas), Dr. Moore spent only four afternoons a week in his office. How did Doggy see more patients than any other doctor in Spruce Harbor?

Very simple. Doggy held office hours everywhere. This annoyed certain people, particularly his golfing companions who objected to Doggy having office hours on the golf course. On an average day Doggy saw one patient per hole. Maybe he'd hold off on a patient on short par threes, but he'd squeeze in an extra one on a par five. He charged the same as for regular office calls, claiming professional effort on the golf course took away from his concentration and caused him to blow a few shots, thereby decreasing his winnings. His opponents, who were always trying to get even on the bets, maintained that the patients bugged their concentration more than Doggy's.

Doggy Moore was one of the few serious golfers anywhere whose golf bag and cart carried throat sticks, flashlight, otoscope, ophthalmoscope, stethoscope, injectable penicillin, a selection of oral antibiotics, sterile gloves, a suture set, a sigmoidoscope, a vaginal speculum and the paraphernalia necessary for obtaining and preserving Papanicolaou smears of the uterine cervix. The sixth hole at Spruce Harbor was known as Doggy's office. There was a shaded, secluded, open but roofed rain shelter with a wide bench which Doggy used for an examining table. It was here that he performed his most definitive golf course examinations. He examined sore bellies, bleeding hemorrhoids and performed occasional pelvic examinations. The Spruce Harbor golfers treated the office with proper respect, but embarrassing situations would occur when the summer complaints were allowed on the course. One male summer complaint found Doggy performing a sigmoidoscopy, that is, an examination of the rectum and sigmoid colon. He never played Spruce Harbor again. Another summer complaint, a matronly female, about a forty handicapper, was off her game for a month after Doggy drafted her to chaperone a pelvic exam on a young lady suspected of an inflammatory disease.

The sixth hole bothered everybody but Doggy. His group, usually two down to Doggy by then, would wait while Doggy practiced medicine. Sometimes they'd have to let another foursome through. Sooner or later Doggy would appear, and yell, "Let's go." He would tee up his Titleist, take his short Doug Sanders swing, put it out two-forty, and say: "Stiddy. Stiddy, ball." The ball always remained steady. Right down the middle. His opponents and even his partners were lucky to hit the ball at all off the sixth tee.

The thing about Doggy Moore was that everyone complained about him, but if they were sick everyone wanted him, any way they could get him. Therefore there were usually five or six patients waiting at the clubhouse when Doggy got in. They didn't like to have their history taken while Doggy simultaneously collected his golf winnings, but they would hold still for it. If Doggy decided to examine a female in the ladies' locker room, the ladies all complained, but the loudest complainer was likely to get examined there a week later.

"Why do I have to see you here, Doggy?" was the wail of all female golfers.

"Go to someone else. You don't have to see me at all. I ain't particular," Doggy would say.

The golf course wasn't Doggy's only extra office work area. When Doggy fished at Chesuncook, folks came in their boats to consult him. When Doggy was rabbit hunting and returned to his truck or station wagon, he'd find patients waiting for him. Doggy played but he was always on duty.

Doggy watched Hawkeye Pierce very carefully. Because Doggy knew everything, he knew all about Hawkeye, his training, his friends, his family. Doggy knew that Hawkeye was going to be the best surgeon in Spruce Harbor, but he held off for a few months. He figured that even though Hawkeye was getting a fast start the rube medical scene might drive him off. Hawkeye might get disgusted and go back to the Cardia Nostra. Doggy sent Hawkeye a few patients, but he checked the deluge of surgery which he could have unleashed. A special situation finally broke the ice between Doggy Moore and Hawkeye Pierce.

On a morning in December, five months after Hawk's arrival in Spruce Harbor, Dr. Moore said to Dr. Pierce: "Boy, do you make house calls?"

"I don't rule them out," Hawkeye said, "but there's not a helluva lot a chest surgeon can do at a house except shake hands and eat unless he gets real lucky."

Doggy gave him a speculative look and asked, "Boy, are you doing anything the rest of the morning?"

"No."

"How about riding out to Hump Hill with me and taking a look at a Finch-Brown?"

"Where is Hump Hill and what is a Finch-Brown?"

"Boy, you may have a big league medical education, but you got a lot to learn. Come with me!"

They rode in Doggy's beat-up four-year-old Chevy station wagon and Doggy started to talk. "Now," he said, "I'm going to tell you about Hump Hill. Hump Hill is ten miles north of Spruce Harbor. It's just a mile or so beyond Hump Flats and it overlooks Hump Pond. It's a sparsely settled area, populated entirely by one of our oldest Maine families, the Finch-Browns. The Finch-Browns have honored me the past thirty-five years by making me their family physician."

"Why do you call it Hump Hill, Hump Pond and Hump Flats?" Hawk asked.

"Because those christly Finch-Browns do nothing but hump, eat and drink, morning, noon and night, and there's more humpin' than there is eatin' and they prefer it anyhow. You may think this is bad, but this community has fewer problems than any other in the state. It may be that the rest of the world should study the Finch-Browns very closely and pattern our civilization after theirs, although I doubt it."

"What problems do they have?"

"As a general rule, only three: poverty, feeblemindedness and venereal disease."

When Doggy talked he liked to look at his audience and Hawkeye was a little nervous about the driving. Nevertheless, he asked another question: "How'd you get to be their doctor?"

"Well, I'll tell you."

"I never doubted it."

"It was over thirty years ago when I first started practice. I had to go down to Fortin's Funeral Home on Front Street. My old friend Johny Fortin still runs it. I had to sign a death certificate. Johnny was busy when I went in and I didn't want to bother him so I looked the place over. Out in the back room I found a coffin and I opened it."

Turning toward Hawkeye and ignoring a pulpwood truck, Doggy asked, "What do you think was in that coffin?"

"Beats me."

"Well, I'll tell you! It was a muskrat!!"

Dr. Pierce had no time to react before Dr. Moore continued, narrowly missing a large fuel oil truck. "Do you know what that muskrat had on?"

"No."

"It had on a goddamn tuxedo. Did you ever see a muskrat wearing a tuxedo?"

"No."

"Neither had I."

"What'd you do then?" Hawk asked.

"Gimme time and I'll tell you. I gotta get past this friggin' snowplow."

He passed it on a blind curve, causing a bulk-feed truck to crash into a snowdrift.

"Well, I went out to the office and I found Johnny and I said, 'Johnny, what kind of a business you running here anyhow? What are you doing with a muskrat dressed up in a tuxedo in that coffin out back?'

" 'Don't be so foolish,' Johnny said. 'That ain't no muskrat. That there's a Finch-Brown, from out back of the moon, out Hump Pond way.'

" 'You don't mean to tell me it was human?' I ask him.

" 'I don't know about that, but it sure as hell was a Finch-Brown.'

" 'Well,' I said, 'I've heard about them all my life, but where in hell did he get a tuxedo?' and Johnny told me it was just the front of a tuxedo he pasted onto him. You ever hear the likes of that?" demanded Dr. Moore.

"No," was all Hawkeye could say as Doggy skidded into the path of another pulp truck.

"How'd you get to be their doctor?" he asked again, after the truck had barely eluded them.

"That's what I'm tryin' to tell you if you'd only keep still."

"Oh."

"It started," continued Doggy, "right there in that funeral parlor. A bunch of people and kids came in and right off I knew they had to be Finch-Browns.

They don't all look like muskrats. Some of them actually more closely resemble chipmunks, but they all have pointed heads with ears that leave at right angles. These are basic characteristics and when you see them you know it's a Finch-Brown, no matter what they look like otherwise. Anyway, one of the smaller ones was making so much noise breathing that I took a close look and every time he breathed his nostrils dilated like he had no good way to get air in or out of him.

"I says to one of the larger ones, 'What ails that one there?' and the larger one kinda grins but don't say nothing', so I muckle onto this kid and I pry his mouth open and look at his throat and he's got tonsils the size of lemons. Now I know you think I'm exaggerating," Doggy said as he skidded across the center line and faked a milk truck into the ditch, "but this kid's tonsils were absolutely as big as lemons, and his adenoids weren't far behind."

"So what'd you do?"

"I turned to the bunch of big muskrats and I said, 'I'm taking this one up to the hospital and I'm going to clean out these tonsils and adenoids before he chokes to death."

"Well," Doggy continued, "this didn't mean anything to them, but I took the kid by the hand and led him out to my car. He was perfectly happy to go. The rest of the muskrats didn't pay any attention. They had a case of beer and were preparing for the funeral. The next day I took the boy's tonsils and adenoids out. The day after that when I went in to see him he was breathing normally, probably for the first time in his life. Then, by Gawd, that night the Finch-Browns showed up at the hospital to see the patient, but they were half in the bag and a lot more interested in looking over the hospital than they were in visiting relatives. When they discovered the flush toilets things got completely out of control."

Doggy dodged a cat, caromed off the snowbank on the wrong side of the road and continued, "When I say completely, I mean completely. For three hours those Finch-Browns did nothing but flush toilets and laugh and scream and holler. They thought a flush toilet was the most remarkable thing they'd ever seen and there's no question about it: it was. I couldn't do anything with them. Finally I hired a couple of taxicabs, loaded the dumb bastards into them and shipped them back to Hump Hill. I told them I'd bring the kid home when he was ready to come.

"The next day and the day after that I went in to see that kid and he just grinned at me. He was probably five or six years old but he couldn't talk worth a damn. After three days I asked him if he wanted to go home and he started to cry. I postponed it another day."

There was a slight catch in Doggy Moore's loud voice. He coughed and lit a cigarette and went on, "I'm married to one of the most *foolish*, and make no mistake, boy, when I say *foolish*, I mean *foolish* females you'll ever run across. She's just as *foolish* today as the day she married me. The afternoon before the day I was definitely going to take that kid back to Hump Hill, she went into the hospital and took him some toys. She spent two hours with him. I went in to see the kid after office hours and he wasn't there. I asked the nurse, 'Where in hell is that chipmunk?'

"Judy Lane, you know her, was running the ward, even back then. 'His mother took him home, Doggy,' says Judy. I tell you I breathed a sigh of relief. I made a house call and got home just in time for supper. As far as I knew all me and that foolish woman had was two kids, but there were three kids at the supper table. Our two and the christless chipmunk."

Doggy coughed and seemed, for a fleeting moment, lost for words.

"Good God!" Hawkeye said.

"Whaddya mean by that?" Doggy asked.

"You know what I mean, Doggy. I knew Chipmunk Moore in college. I always wondered what the story was."

"I thought you must be the kid named Pierce that was Chippy's friend down to Androscoggin College."

"Gentle Jesus, I'll never forget the day he went off to join the air force. Chipmunk Moore and five big rugged football players, and Chippy was the only one who made pilot and the only one who didn't come back. Missing in action in the South Pacific. Right?"

"Yeah, a month before the goddamn war ended," said Doggy. He was quiet for a moment and went on, "We raised him just like he was our own. I don't know whether he was the only Finch-Brown with brains ever produced or whether it was just a change in environment. It doesn't matter. Anyway, now you know why I'm taking you to a house call on Hump Hill."

The old doctor and the young doctor rode in silence for two miles and indulged in their memories. They passed squalid shacks with snow up to the windows, smoke coming from the chimneys and ragged children playing in the road.

"This here's Hump Flats," said Doggy.

"What's this house call all about?" Hawkeye asked.

"There's a kid I want you to look at."

The station wagon climbed Hump Hill and Doggy pulled up in front of a large barnlike structure which looked as though it might collapse at any moment.

"This," announced Doggy, "is the ancestral home of

the Finch-Browns, and incidentally, the birthplace of the late Captain Chipmunk Moore, of the U. S. Army Air Force. Inside you're going to meet Elihu Finch-Brown. He's the Chipmunk's real father."

Doggy opened the door and they entered a large barracks with a dirt floor, furnished with three old wood stoves, rickety chairs and a variety of bunks, beds and dirty mattresses resting upon the floor itself.

"Gawd," said Elihu Finch-Brown, "be that you, Doggy?"

"Who the hell did you think it was, you goddamn moron?" replied Doggy.

"I be some glad to see you, Doggy," replied Elihu. "You got any be-ah?"

"There's a case in the wagon. Help yourself."

"You be a good man, Doggy."

A girl about sixteen ran up and jumped into Doggy's arms. "That medicine fixed me right up, Uncle Doggy," she said. "When you goin' to gimme a try?"

Doggy came out of the depression he'd brought upon himself by talking about his adopted son. His red face got redder, he laughed his big laugh, pushed the girl away, and said, "Never, dearie, but I got a young friend here who could take care of you."

Dearie sort of jumped onto Hawkeye but he shoved her away, a trifle reluctantly. "Forget about me, honey. I'm took," he informed her.

"Elihu," yelled Doggy, "where's that kid with the stove-in chest?"

"Around somewhere," said Elihu, opening a beer. Doggy opened two beers and handed one to Hawkeye.

"Find the kid. Dr. Pierce wants to look at him."

While they awaited the arrival of the kid with the stove-in chest, Dr. Moore proceeded to hold sick call for the Finch-Browns. He handed out antibiotics, punctured two bulging eardrums, and initiated the treatment of two cases of gonorrhea.

Finally the prize patient appeared. A chipmunk. No doubt about it. A chipmunk whose breastbone sort of dove down toward his spine, leaving too little room for heart and hungs. He was a sad specimen.

"Whaddya think of that?" asked Dr. Moore.

"What's this one to Chipmunk Moore?" Hawk asked.

"Nephew, more or less."

"Throw him in your wagon. I can fix him," he said.

Several days later, assisted by Dr. Moore, Hawkeye performed a tedious but successful operation on the young Finch-Brown. After three weeks he wrote the order for his discharge. The boy disappeared from the ward. Two weeks later Hawk met Doggy in the corridor and said, "Hey, Doggy, I oughta see that kid from Hump Hill. Any way to get him in here, or should I take a ride out there?"

"Oh, well," said Doggy. "That won't be any problem. I'll have Emma bring him down to your office. She took him home when you discharged him."

"Who's Emma?"

"Boy, you oughta live in town where you'd hear the news. Emma's the goddamn foolish female I'm married to." Doggy paused for a moment with a faraway look in his eye, pulled himself erect, pointed his finger at Hawkeye and said, "But I want you to know, if she hadn't, I would've."

5

After the trip to Hump Hill and his successful surgery on the young Finch-Brown, Hawkeye caught Doggy Moore's surgical deluge. He was extremely busy and was now a man of substance in the medical community. At one of the daily coffee-shop conferences Tony Holcombe said, "Look, Hawkeye, I know that your office in Wooden Leg's fish factory is free and that Jocko stole all the equipment from the VA. But isn't it time for you to get off the waterfront and find a real office?"

"I hate offices. You're right, of course, but frankly, I like where I am. I almost think I'd stay there if Wooden Leg didn't send every dose of clap in Spruce Harbor for a shot of penicillin. I figured if I taught Shine, that fishscaled clown who works for Wooden Leg, how to give shots I'd drive the trade away, but he's taken to it, and the sufferers have taken Shine to their bosom. So often, in fact, that Shine needs a shot himself about once a week."

"Really, Hawkeye," said Tony, "that's no good. I tell you what. I'm getting more and more patients from Spruce Harbor and I've been thinking of moving in here. Why don't we open an office together?"

"Okay. Where?"

"I don't know. Perhaps your friend Allcock could

make arrangements. He seems good at that sort of thing."

"I expect Jocko will take care of us. This reminds me. I'm just about as busy as I want to be. I've been thinking about trying to find another surgeon. I don't really have enough work to keep two guys busy, but the time will come. Frankly, I'm thinking in terms of you and me and trained people we bring in taking this town over. How's the idea grab you?"

"I'm not sure what you mean."

"Well, we start slowly and feel our way, but the idea is to have someone in every specialty and hope to provide just about every service available in a university hospital. That may sound grandiose, but I think it's possible. Something to shoot for anyway."

"Yes, well, of course. Let's start by getting a decent office and another surgeon, if you feel you can't keep up."

"Jesus, you always put me on the defensive. I want to work and do a good job but I want to play, too. I'm not a guy who'd rather work than anything else. I don't want to own the world or be adored by my segment of it."

"All right then. Find another surgeon."

Dr. Pierce thought for another week about a new surgeon and then wrote to Dr. Augustus Bedford Forrest of Forrest City, Georgia:

Hey Duke,

The last I heard you'd finished your surgical residency and taken a year of urology. Are you in practice, or what? I kid you not, Duke, I got too much surgery and we need a guy who can do urology. What's more, I'm lonely. I have an idea for reuniting the Swampmen. You, me, Trapper John and Spearchucker. We cut it in Korea. Here, as a team, I think we could do a lot of good for the area and for ourselves and have some fun along the way.

Face it Duke, Georgia is too hot. Sherman may return and wipe you out. Now is the time to escape to the rockbound coast of Maine. Don't forget your golf clubs, and bring anything else you need, like wife, kids, etc.

See you around the campus,
Hawk

For three weeks Hawkeye waited to hear from Duke Forrest. It was together with Duke that Hawkeye had arrived, worked at and left the 4077th Mobile Army Surgical Hospital in Korea. It had been five years since Duke and Hawkeye had parted in the men's john of Midway Airport in Chicago.

Then at ten o'clock one morning a six-foot, dark-haired Georgian, slightly heavier than he'd been in Korea, accompanied by a large, efficient-looking bloodhound, entered the Spruce Harbor General Hospital. The first person they met was Dr. Goofus MacDuff. "Can y'all tell me how to find Hawkeye Pierce?" Duke asked.

"I don't think you should bring the dog into the hospital," said Goofus.

"When y'all know it for sure y'all write my mother a letter. Now y'all gonna tell me how to find Hawkeye?"

"He isn't always here. He might be somewhere else. I don't know," said Goofus.

Hawkeye was in the operating room. The word of Duke's arrival filtered slowly to him and he left word for Duke to wait in the coffee shop. Finishing a gallbladder, Doctors Pierce and Holcombe found Duke drinking coffee at a corner table while his bloodhound ate hamburgers from a plate on the floor. Everyone watched them, half in fear, half in curiosity, and kept a respectful distance.

Duke and Hawkeye greeted each other with a handshake and not much else. Each remembered their departure from the 4077th MASH when, momentarily, they'd had lumps in their throats and tears in their eyes.

"This one of your kids?" Hawkeye finally asked.

"Not exactly, but she's better bred. This is Little Eva."

"Is Little Eva part of your act, or are you chasing something?"

"We just get along good," Duke explained. "You got an office for me? I'm a little short. I better get to work soon. My kids gotta eat."

"Oh excuse me, Tony. Duke, this is Tony Holcombe."

"Welcome, Duke. Do I understand you're quite ready to start work?"

"Yep."

"How come?" asked Hawkeye. "I mean, I wanted you to and figured you might show, but I didn't really expect you to haul up stakes so fast."

"I don't understand it either. Can we get Trapper and Spearchucker?"

"I think so, but I'm not sure. I figured if you and I get something going, we could talk them into it. They're both getting to be pretty big cats, but you never know."

"We got an office?"

"Oh dear," said Tony.

"I've just moved out of a fish factory. For a while you and I and Tony are going to share an old office building. Then as soon as it's built, maybe in a year, we're going to move into the Finestkind Clinic and Fishmarket."

"Should I ask specifically about this clinic and fish market, or should I just learn as I go along?"

"It's fairly simple. Jocko Allcock and Wooden Leg Wilcox run a sort of surgical lottery and Wooden Leg is on the board of directors here. They are prospering and are building a large modern office building which can be expanded to accommodate all the talent we want to bring in. We will have the option of buying in or paying rent to Jocko and Wooden Leg. It's going to be right on the shore—a place called Harbor Point. That's a couple of miles out of town and next to where they're going to build our new hospital. I'd say two years away at least."

"Sounds okay," said Duke. "What's this fish market business?"

"Oh, well, Wooden Leg has always wanted a good retail fish market so he figures he'll have one in the clinic. He's going to have a wharf there. The boys can bring their lobsters and clams and shrimp to the clinic. He'll still do the filleting at his wholesale place, I hope."

"Ah can tell it's going to be a real high-class operation in every way," said Duke.

"I sometimes wonder," mused Tony Holcombe.

Jocko Allcock, visiting the hospital to borrow blood for the Veterans Hospital, entered the coffee shop.

"Duke's ready to roll," said Hawkeye. "He does urology in addition to general surgery. Can you find half a dozen prostates for him?"

"No problem," Jocko assured him.

Word of Duke and Little Eva spread through the halls, linen closets and doctors' loitering areas of Spruce Harbor General Hospital. Goofus MacDuff and the good guys made a lively effort to oppose Duke's appointment to the staff. They reasoned that, given an ally, Hawkeye would be unbeatable. Their reasoning was impeccable. Duke, like Hawkeye, was certified by the American Board of Surgery. Wooden Leg Wilcox controlled the board of directors and Duke's application for surgical privileges was quickly approved.

Two months later Duke and Hawkeye, convinced that a neurosurgeon was a Spruce Harbor necessity, went to Philadelphia to interview Dr. Oliver Wendell (Spearchucker) Jones who had been the neurosurgeon and their friend at the 4077th MASH in Korea.

"How we going to play it?" asked Duke.

"Let's get a few laughs. Maybe an act like we put on in Korea when we went to call on that General."

"Y'all think that's wise? Old Spearchucker's just been made boss of that brain factory. He might not go for it."

"Oh, hell, let's have some fun. Let's get you a sheriff's badge and a big hat. That and Little Eva should make them sit up and take notice at University Hospital."

By the time they'd found Spearchucker's office they'd attracted a small but interested crowd. Duke and Hawkeye were getting a mite nervous but Little Eva was steady as a rock. In Dr. Jones's office they found a tall, decorative, redheaded secretary who took one look at them and burst out laughing.

"Look, honey," Duke protested, "you're supposed to be scared. You ain't supposed to laugh. We come to git us a two-hundred-and-thirty-pound buck nigra neurosurgeon."

"Spearchucker around?" asked Hawk.

"He should be just about through in surgery. Would you like me to call him?"

"Yeah," said Hawkeye. "Tell him to get his black ass back here."

"Who shall I say is calling? Just two guys with a bloodhound?"

"Yes."

"And the bloodhound's name, please?"

"Little Eva."

"Of course. What else?"

Just then Dr. Spearchucker Jones called his office and was told: "Doctor, there are two gentlemen and a bloodhound named Little Eva here. They say to tell you to get your black ass back here right away."

"One of them talk south and one north?" Dr. Jones asked.

"I guess."

"Look, Ruby. Don't mind anything they say or do. There's some booze in my lower desk drawer. Give it to them. I'll be there in fifteen or twenty minutes."

"Booze at eleven o'clock in the morning? Yes, sir."

Ruby invited her guests into the inner office and served bourbon and coke. After some small talk, Ruby's curiosity got the better of her.

"Are you guys crazy?" she asked.

"No, I'm Hawkeye Pierce and this is Duke Forrest."

"I should have recognized you. Dr. Jones has a picture of you and another doctor."

"Trapper John."

"Yes, I've met Trapper. He's called several times. In fact, he took me to lunch one day."

"You get anything to eat?" asked Duke.

"Trapper still work fast?" asked Hawkeye.

"Now look. I'm very happily married to Dr. Jones's chief resident and he's just as big as Dr. Jones, so you keep civil tongues in your heads or I'll have you taken care of."

"I'll sic mah dog on you," Duke mumbled.

"Pretty tough broad," observed Hawkeye.

"Oh, knock it off," suggested Ruby. "What do you guys want?"

"We want a neurosurgeon in Spruce Harbor, Maine, and therefore we want to liberate Spearchucker from the ghetto and bring him to Spruce Harbor."

"Dr. Jones hardly lives in the ghetto. He's the youngest head of a neurosurgical department in the country. Do you seriously think he'd give this up to go to some country town?"

"Why not?" asked Hawkeye. "Wait'll he hears about the Finestkind Clinic and Fishmarket."

"Yeah, wait," said Duke.

"Hey, Ruby," Hawkeye interrupted. "You got nothing to worry about. If we can't get the coon we'll grab your husband. He must be okay or Spearchucker wouldn't have him around."

Ruby seemed unable to react.

"Little Eva is hungry," Duke announced. "You couldn't send out for a steak or something?"

Dr. Oliver Wendell Jones arrived before Ruby could order lunch for Little Eva. "Well, Ruby," he said, "I expect you've been subjected to sexual propositions, comments upon cities in general and Philadelphia in particular, as well as a variety of racist remarks."

"Hawkeye called you a coon only once, sir," said Ruby.

"That's right. You folks always stick together. Hey, little white boy," he said to Duke, "I'm glad to see you."

"Same here, Chucker. That's why we came. We can't get along without you."

"Let's go to lunch," suggested Dr. Jones. "Come along, Ruby, and get an idea of what crazy people are like."

Over the first martini, Hawkeye said: "Look, Chucker, let's get it over with. You're a big deal here in the city. Whoopee. Christ, you may be the best in one part of Philly but there's ten guys around who could take your job and do it if you get hit by a truck. You're living in a goddamn five-hundred-a-month apartment I wouldn't be caught dead in and your kids are growing up with no breathing room. In Spruce Harbor we'll see you make as much money. You'll be providing a service that you can't fulfill and supply here. We need a neurosurgeon. There's no way for you to stay in the city unless you just want to be a big professor and go from meeting to meeting bullshitting everybody."

"You're forgetting my color," said Spearchucker softly.

"How could I forget it?" asked Hawkeye. "You're blacker'n hell, but what's your point?"

"Two points, Hawk. One, there's going to be resistance to a black neurosurgeon in Spruce Harbor and two, I would be copping out if I went to Spruce Harbor. You know what I mean. I'm a nationally known ex-athlete and a neurosurgeon. If I go to Spruce Harbor I'll get all kinds of heat. I have a responsibility to my people."

"Let's take your two points, one at a time," said Hawk. "There is no great desire in Spruce Harbor for a black neurosurgeon, but the majority of the medical profession dislike us so much that they'd accept you, even beg you to come if they thought they'd be shafting Duke and Hawkeye. In fact, Duke and I may be a trifle antagonistic when you first visit Spruce Harbor. As for the second point, that's a matter of philosophy and we've been through it before. As far as I'm concerned we should be human beings first and colors second, so if you want to major in color, stay in

Philadelphia. If you want to come to Spruce Harbor, you may, by example and performance, do more for human beings of all colors than you can here. It's your pop, babe."

"We'll have watermelons shipped in on the underground railroad," offered Duke, just before Ruby kicked him in the shins beneath the table.

Before leaving Philadelphia, Duke gave Spearchucker his briefcase and made him promise to bring it to Spruce Harbor. Dr. Jones did not commit himself but Duke and Hawkeye were pretty sure they'd lined up a neurosurgeon.

A week later Dr. Goofus MacDuff, the Medical Director, received a letter from Dr. Oliver Wendell Jones, Chairman of the Department of Neurosurgery at University Hospital in Philadelphia. Dr. Jones's letter stated that he had decided to leave Philadelphia and hoped to practice neurosurgery in a nonurban area of the Northeast. Dr. Jones stated that he was non-Caucasian and hinted that this was a reason for seeking escape from the city. His credentials, in fact and on paper, were more impressive than Hawkeye's or Duke's. Even Goofus MacDuff, nudged by a reference to football in Dr. Jones's letter, was aware of Spearchucker Jones, all-pro fullback in 1954.

Suddenly, to Goofus and the good guys, this letter from Oliver Wendell Spearchucker Jones looked like a great big gold nugget with which they'd bust the skulls of Hawkeye Pierce and Duke Forrest. They answered Dr. Jones's letter and urged him to visit Spruce Harbor.

Spearchucker's visit to Spruce Harbor was announced in advance by the *Spruce Harbor Courier*. The Chamber of Commerce appointed a welcoming committee. The Rotary Club postponed its weekly meeting from Monday till Wednesday so that Spearchucker could address them.

Lucinda Lively, Hawkeye's new secretary—a medium in most ways like height and weight, dog-loving, sex-oozing twenty-three-year-old blonde—and Little Eva also met Spearchucker when he arrived at Spruce Harbor Airport. Spearchucker's plane landed at 11:20 A.M. on Wednesday morning. He was welcomed by Goofus and the President of the Chamber of Commerce and the President of the Rotary Club, which Dr. Jones would address at noon. Bloodhounds have a particularly keen sense of smell. As Lucinda Lively and Little Eva followed the famous man into the small terminal, Little Eva caught a scent. She strained at her leash and, it seemed to the audience, had an overpowering desire to possess Dr. Oliver Wendell Jones. Of course Little Eva had already met Dr. Jones and considered him a friend and Dr. Jones was carrying a briefcase lent him by Dr. Duke Forrest.

Little Eva's effort to greet her friend was restrained by Lucinda Lively who, in fact, needed help from the audience. Dr. Jones's reaction, later described in the *Spruce Harbor Courier* as one of fear and anger, was actually a barely successful effort to suppress laughter.

The newspaper account proclaimed that "the famous Negro athlete and brain surgeon, Dr. Oliver Jones, was attacked by a bloodhound upon his arrival in Spruce Harbor," and explained that the bloodhound was owned by Dr. Augustus Forrest, who had recently moved to Spruce Harbor from Georgia. In an editorial, the editor hoped that "racial prejudice will never raise its ugly head in Spruce Harbor, Maine." He added that Dr. Jones was considering the practice of neurosurgery in Spruce Harbor and urged the community to spare no effort in convincing Dr. Jones that his future lay in Spruce Harbor.

After addressing the Rotary Club, whose members concentrated on questions about football, and after a difficult afternoon with Goofus and the good guys, Spearchucker Jones was allowed to check into his room at the Spruce Harbor Motel. Goofus, although he'd considered inviting Spearchucker to his home, thought better of it. With a great sigh of relief, Spearchucker said aloud, to himself: "What a day. I'm going to have a shower and a nice big drink of bourbon before I have to face that gang tonight."

"Could you make it two bourbons, Spearchucker?" said another voice.

Before Dr. Jones could answer, Little Eva shyly but sincerely paid her respects. "I'm Lucinda Lively, Hawkeye's secretary," explained the other voice from a sofa next to the TV set.

Spearchucker assessed the quite satisfactory blonde while he fondled Little Eva and laughed. He laughed so long that Lucinda Lively had to interrupt: "Spearchucker, may I please have a drink? I hope you don't mind my calling you that. Use of last names is considered discourteous around here."

"What are you doing here, Lucinda?"

"Hawkeye sent me. I'm a problem to him. He hopes you'll take me to bed, but I'm not going to let you."

"Oh. May I ask why?"

"Nothing personal. It's just that I'm twenty-three and I don't plan to marry until I'm twenty-seven and I don't want to acquire a reputation for sleeping around."

"Uh-huh," said Dr. Jones.

"What's Trapper John like?" asked Lucinda.

"He's like them. Maybe worse. Why?"

"Because I think Hawkeye's master plan is to use

me for bait so he can get Trapper to come to Spruce Harbor."

"Nice bait. Let's have a drink, Lucinda. By the way, how'd you and Little Eva get in here?"

"Oh, I have lots of ways," said Lucinda.

"I'm supposed to go to a staff meeting at the hospital tonight," said Dr. Jones.

"And a party at Dr. MacDuff's afterward," said Lucinda. "You'd better have three bourbons. Hawkeye and Duke and Tony Holcombe are not going to be very cordial. I guess you know that."

"Yes. Do they have definite plans or are they just going to be spontaneous?"

"Well," said Lucinda, "Hawkeye has a big bullwhip that's been lying around his father's barn for fifty years and Duke has a rope with a hangman's noose on one end of it. Whip and noose are displayed, conspicuously, in their station wagons. And I heard them discussing the propriety of burning a fiery cross somewhere, perhaps in front of the motel."

"My God," moaned Spearchucker. "Do you think I should cut out tonight?"

"No. I don't think they're going to carry it too far. It's just that they have juvenile minds and this gives them a chance to let their imaginations run wild. If they overdo it, they'll spoil it and they want you so bad they can taste it."

"You really think they do, Lucinda?"

"Yes, sir, I know they do. I always call doctors 'sir' when the discussion gets serious."

"Why do you think they want me? There are lots of neurosurgeons. Because I was a football player and they happen to know me?"

Lucinda sat up straight, leaned forward in her chair and said: "No, sir. I don't understand it completely and I haven't known Duke and Hawkeye very long, but if they want you, they want you."

"Lucinda, are you in love with Hawkeye?"

"I don't know. If I am, it has no future, so what difference does it make? I'll take a long look at Trapper John, if he ever comes."

"He'll come, Lucinda."

"How about you, Spearchucker?"

"Probably I will. Now you and that animal get out of here before the White Citizens Council catches me in here with a white girl."

After Lucinda Lively and Little Eva left his room in the Spruce Harbor Motel, Dr. Jones tried to do some careful thinking. One afternoon with Goofus MacDuff and the good guys had confirmed what his friends had said about them. One was dumb and the others were phonies and they wanted him not for the benefit of the community but to help fight or contain Pierce and Forrest. But what about friends? Dr. Jones knew that there would be enough work and he'd make a good living. He knew that Duke and Hawkeye wanted him because he was their friend and that, up to a point, they were color-blind. He remembered, though, Hawk's response in Korea to, "Why do you cut out so often when my friends come to visit me?" Hawk had said: "Do you like all the white boys around here?"

Dr. Jones had many friends of all colors but, mostly, they were black. He knew that Duke and Hawkeye were opinionated, arbitrary screwballs. But how, he wondered, would they swing if he did as they suggested and tried to bring other blacks into Maine? Would they overlook the occasional loser, the bad choice, or would they say, as Hawkeye had in the past: "Live human, or live colored, and don't bomb us with wrong niggers."

As Spearchucker Jones stepped out of his shower

and picked up the bourbon and coke he'd left on the washstand, he decided: I'm going to do it. These guys are crazy, but I hate the city, too. If they like me as much as they seem to, they'll go along with my need to be a nigger. So relax, Jonesy, and roll along and see what happens. The kids will love it around here.

The staff meeting at Spruce Harbor General Hospital always began with the reading of the minutes of the last meeting and a listing of those who had attended the last meeting. Class D ball, thought Spearchucker. Maybe I'll change my mind. Goofus MacDuff presided over a variety of nonprofessional, irrational, pointless reports before announcing that the clinical meeting (which always was secondary to the nonsense) would be postponed in favor of a party at his house where everyone could meet Dr. Oliver Wendell Jones.

At the party, Spearchucker heard Duke Forrest say, "Y'all just don't understand nigras," and Dr. Tony Holcombe's comment was, "Can you imagine that bloody great savage rummaging around in one's brain?"

When Dr. Jones left Spruce Harbor on Thursday, he thanked Doctors MacDuff, Coffin and the other good guys for their hospitality and said: "Gentlemen, I've already reached a decision. I am coming to Spruce Harbor. I appreciate your kind offer to join you gentlemen in practice but Doctors Pierce, Forrest and Holcombe have convinced me that my future lies with the Finestkind Clinic and Fishmarket."

Goofus and the good guys were quite hung up. They didn't know how it had happened, but they got the word. They'd been had.

6

Dr. and Mrs. Pierce had, with money borrowed from Jocko and Wooden Leg, built a big new house in Crabapple Cove, a few yards inland from the tide-lapped quarters they had first occupied. Duke and Sandra Forrest bought an old farm half a mile farther down Pierce Road and rebuilt it, nearly from the ground up. Duke and Hawkeye thought Spearchucker should also live in Crabapple Cove, but Jocko vetoed this idea.

"No. That wouldn't be no good," said Jocko. "Wooden Leg's gettin' him that old Howard place that's been fixed up down on Harbor Point right near where the clinic and hospital's going to be. Him and his kids shouldn't be way out. They gotta be normal. You and Duke is crazy so it don't matter."

Jocko Allcock, as a VA employee with clinical awareness, knew where to find any number of ruptured intervertebral discs which the VA couldn't or wouldn't handle, as well as a variety of other potential neurosurgical problems. Spearchucker Jones's first month in Spruce Harbor was very busy.

The Pierces and Forrests were always socially backward, but a month after Spearchucker and Evelyn Jones arrived, they were invited to a welcome party at the Pierces'. They'd already been to several large parties given by doctors and other prominent citizens where the Pierces and Forrests, although invited, had not appeared.

The Pierce-Forrest party was small, attended only by the hosts, the guests of honor, Jocko Allcock, the Wilcoxes, and Big Benjy Pierce, who was pressed into service as bartender and cook until he passed out. Spearchucker, of course, had visited Crabapple Cove before but had never happened to meet Big Benjy, whose reaction, even before the introduction, was, "Jesus Christ, ain't he a big one? I'd sure hate to have him muckle onto me."

"Keep a civil tongue in your head, you old bastard," said Hawkeye, "or I'll see that he does muckle onto you. Spearchucker, I'd like you to meet my father."

"I'm happy to meet you, Mr. Pierce. I've heard a lot about you."

"Gawd, boy, I guess I'm some proud to meetcha," answered Big Benjy. "I tell you my boy was sure some happy when you come down heah to work. How you likin' it?"

"Oh, finestkind," said Spearchucker, with a straight face and a slight twinkle of the eye.

Before Spearchucker's arrival in Spruce Harbor, Hawkeye had feared the possible consequences, in terms of local morbidity and mortality, of Dr. Jones's being addressed as "boy." He had planned to warn Dr. Jones but later decided to wait and see what happened. Nothing happened except that, more and more, Spearchucker addressed others as "boy."

"You seem to be falling into the local vernacular, Chucker," observed Hawkeye one day.

"At first I didn't understand and came damn close to coldcocking a citizen or two but I caught on in time. What I dread is the possibility of, eventually, being addressed as 'young fella.' "

"I don't get it."

"Haven't you noticed? Around here one is greeted with 'Hi, boy' until the age of seventy. Then the greeting is changed to 'Hi there, young fella.' "

Spearchucker's wife Evelyn cornered Jocko Allcock. She was curious about him and the surgical lottery and she was well aware that Jocko was responsible for the initial flood of patients.

"Where on earth do you dig up all these ruptured discs, Mr. Allcock?"

"Jocko, ma'am, if you don't mind."

"All right. Jocko it is, and I'm Evelyn."

"Well, Evelyn, I work for the VA and I know lots of people, so it ain't hard to put my finger on plenty of stuff when a new boy comes in. I tell you, me and Wooden Leg been makin' good money. Just like when Hawkeye come. Everybody's sure these fancy specialists are goin' to knock 'em off right and left and Jonesy ain't had no trouble so we're cleanin' up."

"Jocko, I thought there might be some resistance. I wasn't sure Oliver would be accepted by the patients, particularly at first."

"Oliver? Oh, you mean the Chucker. Hell, no. Only trouble I had was with some folks over to Tedium Cove thought he might be related to them Joneses they got over theah. Worst bunch you ever see."

The party was relatively quiet except that Big Benjy got loaded on Scotch and wanted to fight Spearchucker, just because Big Benjy, when he wants to fight, always picks the biggest guy around. Jimmy and Alice Richards dropped in for a drink and to meet the Joneses. Jimmy, an old high school classmate of Hawkeye's, was the druggist in Port Waldo and daylighted, in summer, as pro at the Wawenock Harbor Country Club where he and Hawkeye had caddied as kids. After the Richardses left, Spearchucker said,

"I'm probably going to have your friend Jimmy as a patient pretty soon."

"Why?"

"You didn't notice his right leg? A couple of times it twitched and he couldn't control it. He was scared as hell."

"No. I didn't notice. What do you think it means?"

"Any number of things or nothing. Let's wait and see."

The wait wasn't long. At ten fifteen the next morning, with ten people in the drugstore, Jimmy Richards fell to the floor, gasping for breath, his whole right side involved in a violent, uncontrollable convulsion. Dr. Ralph Young arrived in time to see the tag end of it. There was nothing he could do.

"I'll call Hawkeye," he said. Finding Pierce at Spruce Harbor General, Dr. Young described the situation as best he could.

"Throw him in Jack Leeman's hearse and whistle him over here," advised Hawkeye. "This sounds like work for the Spearchucker."

In November Jimmy Richards had gone up-country, deer hunting. After tramping over three miles of wooded hills he had a sensation of numbness in his right leg. Leaning against a tree, he massaged the leg, which began to twitch and turn inward. Within seconds the spasm was over. Half an hour later Jimmy shot a one-hundred-and-eighty-pound buck and forgot about his leg.

In early December there was a spell of warm weather. One Sunday morning Jimmy went to the golf course, walked down the first fairway and across the green into the woods, looking for lost golf balls. As he bent to pick one up, his right leg began to shake. Just as in the drugstore, the convulsion spread upward and involved his whole right side. This time it lasted a full minute, leaving Jimmy breathless, frightened and completely exhausted. For a time, his right leg and thigh were paralyzed, but he stumbled and fell until he reached his car. Sensation and motion returned slowly and he drove home. After a stiff drink he felt perfectly well and watched the Giants and Packers on TV.

At Spruce Harbor, after the drugstore episode, Dr. Jones went to work. A spinal tap showed some elevation of pressure in the spinal fluid. An electroencephalogram, a brain-wave test, was of no help. The neurological findings were all within normal limits. Spearchucker decided to do a cerebral arteriogram, which means he injected dye into the carotid artery in the neck and took pictures of the dye as it went through the arteries in the brain.

Jimmy had the kind of head which sat right on his shoulders with little or no neck in between. Spearchucker blew the shot. He couldn't get the dye in the right place, but he did cause some bleeding. He decided to wait two weeks for the swelling to go down before repeating the test. He prescribed a sedative and sent Jimmy home.

This was during Christmas and New Year's and Hawkeye was avoiding all but mandatory work. He visited Jimmy Richards every day. Many citizens of Port Waldo, although aware of Hawkeye's increasing reputation as a surgeon, were wary of him because of his family background, namely Big Benjy Pierce. Now, however, they were impressed by his concern for Jimmy Richards. The public did not know that most of the visits were spent drinking and haggling over football bets or that Dr. Pierce took Jimmy for sixty-eight dollars in ten days. The sedation prevented all but one mild recurrence of the convulsion. Jimmy looked better and better, but Hawkeye Pierce looked worse because he'd decided, in his own mind, that Jimmy had a brain tumor. So had everyone else but with less reason. Jimmy was a popular guy. The Lions' Club, the Rotary Club, the Masons, all came with gifts, flowers and good wishes.

At 1:30 P.M. on the day of the NFL playoff, Dr. Pierce called on Jimmy. There were fifteen people in the living room and gifts from every organization in town. Hawkeye said, "Jimmy, it's a christly insult. The NAACP ain't sent you a thing."

The Methodist minister and two others who for some reason didn't like Dr. Pierce departed hurriedly. That left a dozen. Jimmy, panic-stricken, took Hawkeye aside.

"What am I going to do? I don't want to seem ungrateful, but if they don't leave I won't be able to watch the game."

"Pitch a fit," suggested Hawkeye.

Doing it from memory Jimmy Richards had another attack. Hawkeye considered it a rather poor performance, but most of the guests found it quite convincing. Those who didn't left precipitously when Dr. Pierce, brandishing a pocket knife, held it to Jimmy's neck and announced, "I guess I better do a tracheotomy."

On January 2, Hawkeye took Jimmy back to Spruce Harbor. Most of the tests were repeated and a week later Dr. Jones, with Pierce assisting, exposed the carotid artery in Jimmy's left neck, injected dye and got good X-rays. They showed possible block of one small artery in the brain but did nothing to establish the diagnosis of a brain tumor. The next day Spearchucker explained to Jimmy and Hawkeye that he could neither make a positive diagnosis of brain tumor nor rule it out. However, if there were a tumor, it was so situated that a surgical exploration of that part of the brain would produce weakness or paralysis of the whole right side. Therefore he felt that the most reasonable course was to increase sedation and await further developments. He suggested two more weeks of rest. If there were no convulsions, the patient could gradually return to work.

Again Dr. Pierce took Mr. Richards home to Port Waldo, where they opened a bottle of Scotch and had a drink. Jenny, Jimmy's wife, came home from the store all upset. Two people had told her how sorry they were that Jimmy had an incurable brain tumor. She'd given them a good answer: "The doctors aren't at all sure of that. If you have special information, you should certainly inform Dr. Jones at Spruce Harbor General."

Then Hawkeye made a speech: "Jimbo, I think your case had been handled very well by the Spearchucker. He's left you on the hook, I admit, but with good reason. All the signs are favorable and he's been completely honest with you. You understand your problem as well as your doctors do. However, whether you realize it or not, Port Waldo has written you off. Uninformed small-town gossip is malignant and uncontrollable. You'll overhear all kinds of stupid opinions and a lot of dumb things are going to be said right to your face. You gotta roll with it, buddy, and remember that you and the gourdcracker are the only two authorities on your illness."

Jimmy was relieved or tried to be. "Let's have another drink," he suggested.

During the second drink, Pierce's mouth started running again: "Jim, old buddy, what I just said is so damned true that some people aren't going to be happy if you go ahead and get well. The Lions' Club may make you pay for the flowers. I think you'd better take advantage of the situation."

Dr. Pierce usually stopped in Port Waldo to buy a paper on nights when he could come home to Crabapple Cove. Twice in the next few days people cornered him and asked questions about Jim Richards. On each occasion he answered the questions warily, hinted that Jimmy's future behavior might be peculiar and expressed the hope that people would be tolerant of it.

Two weeks after his release from the hospital, Jimmy returned to work in the drugstore. At eleven o'clock in the morning he retired to the drug room and, a few minutes later, reappeared behind the soda fountain clad in a jockstrap. He was happy and convivial. No one knew what to do. Dr. Ralph Young was out on a call. Joe Moody, editor of the *Port Waldo Press,* engaged Jimmy in conversation.

"Why are you going around in the jockstrap, Jim?" he asked politely.

"Because the girls like me better this way," Jim explained, looking interestedly at the two young village matrons who were looking interestedly at him.

"Jim, let's go in the drug room and talk this over. I think you oughta get dressed."

Jimmy kept looking at the two young matrons of the village.

Joe Moody went to the phone, called Dr. Pierce and defined the situation as concisely as he could.

"I don't seem to understand the problem," said Hawkeye. "You say Jimmy's got nothing on but a jockstrap and he's eyeing a couple broads. I been watchin' those two myself. Lemme know how he makes out."

Suddenly, Jim Richards vaulted over the soda fountain. The two young village matrons scurried out the door, with the druggist in pursuit. Billy Jordan, the state cop, arrived and, with Joe Moody's help, got Jimmy into the cruiser and took him home.

This was accepted in the village as a manifestation of Jim's brain tumor. There was no criticism. Only pity.

Jimmy's business increased. Curiosity brought customers who hoped to observe unusual behavior. On a Saturday afternoon Jim arrived at the store, climbed onto the soda fountain bar brandishing an iron skillet, and announced to the gathering crowd, "I'm going to kill Hawkeye Pierce."

On cue, Hawkeye walked in. Jimmy jumped from the counter and Hawkeye went out the door with Jim right on his heels, swearing and swinging the skillet. Before anyone could react, victim and assailant had turned a corner and disappeared. Billy Jordan arrived quickly. He and Joe Moody rode around for a while but found no trace of them, so they decided to go to Jimmy' house. Jimmy and the unmurdered physician were drinking Scotch whiskey and watching a golf tournament on television.

"Come in, boys, but keep it quiet. Player's putting for a bird," said Hawkeye. "The booze is in the kitchen. Help yourselves."

Trooper Jordan started to ask a question just as Gary Player stroked his putt. Jimmy looked menacingly at the state policeman.

As the golfers walked to the next tee, Dr. Pierce asked, "You guys got a problem? You look worried."

"We can't have Jimmy chasing people. Somebody's gotta do something about him," declared Billy Jordan.

"Like what? Put him in jail? He wasn't chasing people. He was only chasing me. It so happens I like to be chased by guys with a skillet. I'm strange that way. Anyway, I've had half a step on Jimmy ever since we were in high school."

Dr. Ralph Young appeared and was brought up to date by Billy Jordan.

"Okay," he said. "I don't know what you two are up to, but I can make an educated guess. I'll tell you what's next. You have three choices: Jimmy goes back to the clinic, he goes to the State Fool Farm or you knock off this foolishness right here and now."

"Ralph, old boyhood hero," said Dr. Pierce, "you ain't gonna send a man with a brain tumor to the Fool Farm?"

Ralph asked Trooper Jordan to leave and assured him that he'd get the situation under control. By this time he was beginning to get the idea and had a drink. Mr. Richards and Dr. Pierce laughed again. Dr. Young got mad. "Hawkeye," he said, "what's wrong with you? I know this was your idea. How can you do it?"

"What the hell do you mean, how can I do it? Whenever anyone in this town gets real sick, the grunts have a Roman holiday. We are just catering to their tastes. Do you realize that, as a result of our labors, a hundred housewives will be happy for a whole week? And their husbands will be happy, and their children will be happy? We are contributing to the morale of the whole county. Criticism from a man of your stature ill becomes you."

Dr. Ralph Young, although one of the most respected men in Wawenock County, has never been accused of being a stick-in-the-mud. He sipped his drink reflectively, puffed a cigar and asked, "Okay, what's our next move?"

"Let's hold off till Jimmy goes to the clinic for his checkup," suggested Hawkeye. "That's another couple weeks. We'll have time to make plans. Taking him back to Spruce Harbor will soothe public indignation and allow for maximum enjoyment of the next attack."

Two weeks later snow began late Saturday afternoon and continued all night. By morning, eighteen inches had fallen. Mr. James Richards, druggist and golf pro, went to his store at nine o'clock Sunday morning. He arrived on a sled, hauled by a team of huskies. Cradled in his arm was a shotgun. An hour later, Dr. Pierce, having braved the drifting snow and driven up from Crabapple Cove to get the Sunday *Telegram,* walked into the drugstore. Jimmy grabbed the shotgun. Hawkeye ran down the main street. Jimmy leaped onto the dog sled and took off in hot pursuit. He fired once. Hawkeye rolled in the snow but got up. Jim fired again. Dr. Pierce fell again and didn't get up. Jimmy loaded him aboard the sled and to the gathering throng he announced, "Got him this time. No question about it." Jimmy, the dog team and their grisly cargo disappeared into the storm.

A mile down the road the dogs were returned to their owner, and Hawkeye drove Jim to Spruce Harbor.

Again a search was instituted by concerned citizens, who found Hawkeye Pierce ice fishing on Muscongus Lake that afternoon.

"Took two slugs through the heart, but I heal fast," Hawk informed them.

The Methodist minister stepped forward. "I demand an explanation of this," he demanded.

"Well, that's right neighborly of you, Parson, but I'm not in a conversational mood. If you got a complaint, why don't you see the chaplain?"

"Dr. Pierce, I want to know what this is all about," Reverend Fraser insisted.

"Beats me, Dad," was all the answer he got from Dr. Pierce, who pulled up a big pickerel.

A week later Jimmy came home, off all medication. Further tests revealed nothing that was either diagnostic or frightening. Spearchucker could not explain the previous trouble but hoped, in a doubtful way, that a brain tumor was no longer a possibility. Word filtered back that Jimmy had undergone dangerous but highly effective treatment and would soon be well.

Hawkeye Pierce was interrogated whenever he appeared locally. "How's Jimmy?" he was asked one night in the drugstore.

"He's gonna be okay. The problem's solved."

"What'd they do?"

"They found the trouble was all in his umbilicus and removed it. Always works in this kind of case."

"Will that affect him in any way?" asked the Port Waldo librarian, an authority on medical subjects.

"Sure as hell will, Agnes," Hawkeye assured her. "If he wants to eat celery in bed, he'll have to find another place to put the salt!"

Hawkeye and Spearchucker discussed Jimmy Richards till he came out of their ears and the only answer, in view of negative or equivocal findings and good response to nondescript medication, was: Wait and see. They waited till April and then Jimmy had another convulsion. A bad one. Back to Spruce Harbor General he went and all the tests were repeated. This time the arteriogram was less normal than before but still not abnormal in a definitive way.

The whole gang, Pierce, Jones, Forrest and Holcombe hacked it over in the coffee shop one morning. Spearchucker kept saying, "If I go to where that arteriogram says to go in his brain, I'm going to screw up his golf swing. I have to admit, I just don't know what to do. Maybe we should send him to Boston."

"I've already suggested that to Jimmy," said Hawkeye. "His reply, and I quote him verbatim, was, 'I'm gonna stick with the nigger.' I'm sure you are touched."

"Deeply."

"Perhaps," offered Tony Holcombe, "we should do a GM test."

"What is that?" asked Spearchucker, while Hawkeye and Duke pondered the idea.

"A consultation with Goofus MacDuff. He loves to be called in consultation and really gives it his all and invariably comes up with the wrong answer. The trick is to get his recommendation and then do precisely the opposite."

"I don't know," mused Dr. Pierce. "The Goofus test has always worked out pretty well, but we've used it as kind of a joke. The idea doesn't quite grab me in this case."

"Let me tell y'all something," said Duke, who'd been very quiet up until now. "Goofus is one-eighth genius and seven-eighths moron. Every now and then the genius part comes out and Goofus touches every base until he comes to home plate, which he misses by an inch. He can, and I wouldn't believe it at first, be smart for a while before the moron takes over. Let's do the GM test."

Dr. Goofus MacDuff was asked to see Jimmy Richards who submitted to this investigation only because of his lifelong friendship with Hawkeye Pierce. Goofus devoted the best part of three days to reviewing the case and the literature on the subject and examining the patient. Then he dictated a four-page consultation.

"I wouldn't have believed it," said Spearchucker after two readings. "I just wouldn't have believed it."

"Why?" asked Hawk.

"This guy has done a beautiful job of analyzing and defining this case."

"But in the last paragraph," said Hawkeye, "I guarantee he blew it. What'd he recommend?"

"Conservative treatment. No surgery."

"Put Jimmy on the schedule, Chucker. Let's crack his goddamn head open and get it over with."

Spearchucker removed a deeply situated benign tumor from the left side of Jimmy's brain. This stopped the convulsions but left Jimmy partially paralyzed on the right side. Dr. Jones could not predict how much coordination would return but definitely stated that with time, physiotherapy and determination, there was hope of improvement.

But Dr. Jones did not fully understand that Jimmy Richards was on this earth only to play golf. By mid-August Mr. Richards, although still riding the golf cart, could walk from the golf cart to the ball and hit the ball well enough to break ninety. This was a physical and psychic breakthrough for Jimmy. Always a competitor, he wanted to play Hawkeye a buck Nassau if Hawkeye would give him three shots a side.

"I'll never give a pro strokes," said Hawkeye. "I don't care if you had six brain tumors."

7

As the opening of the Finestkind Clinic and Fishmarket grew closer, Hawkeye, Duke and Spearchucker did all they could to lure Trapper John McIntyre into the Spruce Harbor web. Trapper, at first, wouldn't even listen, but he did visit occasionally and there were hints that he could be reached. Late one night, perhaps overcome by nostalgia he said: "You guys find the dough to build a cardiovascular surgical unit into your new hospital and find me a good-looking broad and I'll give it some thought."

Hawkeye figured he had the broad, Lucinda Lively, but how to get enough money to put Trapper in business was something else. He considered the Allcock-Wilcox gambling syndicate but rejected it as a source of cash. Cardiac surgery was still too risky to make book on. One day in March he had lunch with George Cogswell of the Hamilton Foundation, a Boston-based philanthropy which provided money for medical progress in northern, rural New England. George, the foundation's traveling money-dispenser, had provided a big bundle for the new Spruce Harbor General Hospital because, he told his superiors, Spruce Harbor had several highly trained young specialists and more would come.

George Cogswell and Hawkeye were good friends. George, who had spent one summer as pro at a small club in New Hampshire, always had his golf clubs with him and usually beat Hawkeye, but Hawkeye didn't mind because every time he played with George he conned him for more money for the new hospital.

At this March luncheon, Hawkeye said: "George, if you'll pop for another two hundred grand, we can get one of the country's best young heart surgeons to come to Spruce Harbor. How about it?"

"Don't be ridiculous," said George. "You couldn't possibly find the cases. You'd need at least fifty a year. Oh, Hawkeye, it's out of the question."

"Baby, nothing's out of the question. I'll get to you, but let it go for now."

That evening on his way home to Crabapple Cove, Hawkeye picked up a hitchhiker, his great-uncle Lewis Pierce, a seventy-year-old lobsterman who lived in The Solid Rust Cadillac at the very end of Pierce Road and on the very edge of the Medomak River. In 1959, to the best of anyone's knowledge, Mr. Pierce was the only citizen of the State of Maine living in a 1940 Cadillac. Mr. Pierce had lost his license for drunken driving in 1956 but continued to drive until 1958 when, almost simultaneously, his shack burned to the ground and the Cadillac gave up. Lewis Pierce pushed it down to the shore, at the head of his wharf, and moved in. He shared the Cadillac with selected seagulls. Mr. Pierce and seagulls got along very well.

Most seventy-year-old lobstermen are just seventy-year-old lobstermen, but Lewis Pierce has an alter ego. An eleven handicapper, he is a charter member of the Wawenock Harbor Golf Club where he is known as Lew the Jew. There are several theories about the name. When Hawkeye was very young he theorized that the membership, having no Jews to exclude but nurturing unrequited and at the same time a somewhat guilty feeling of anti-Semitism, had appointed his Uncle Lewis as the Club Jew, thereby serving an emotional need. As time went by, Hawkeye decided that the membership simply liked euphonious names. Whatever the reason, Lewis Pierce was known to the elite of golf throughout Maine as Lew the Jew and to his golfing intimates he was just plain "Jew."

"Hi, Jew," said Hawkeye, as his great-uncle settled down beside him. "How they goin'?"

"Finestkind. By Jesus, this weather keeps up we'll soon be out theah."

"That reminds me, Uncle. Last year I was giving you three shots every nine holes and I was losing money. You figure I'm rich because I'm a doctor, but nobody in his right mind would give you three shots and this year I'll give you two at the most."

"I'll make a deal with yuh," replied Lew the Jew. "I'm gittin' tired of all the talk about how I ain't dressed like no real golfer. You git me some fancy golf clothes and I'll play you for just two shots."

Hawkeye agreed to consider his uncle's request and Saturday afternoon he found in his attic: a pair of yellow Bermuda shorts, a multicolored striped shirt that may have been made out of a beer joint tablecloth, a pair of purple golf shoes with big anterior flaps (donated by a grateful but misguided patient) and a round tasseled tartan golf cap. In all, an ensemble which might go unnoticed at Kiamesha Lake but would get a man put away at the Wawenock Harbor Golf Course. Hawkeye and Big Benjy Pierce visited Uncle Lewis to deliver the clothes. Big Benjy had a fifth of Old Bantam whiskey to which he and Lew the Jew gave their undivided attention, so Hawkeye left.

That night Port Waldo, a political affiliate of Crabapple Cove, had a town meeting. Town meeting always comes at the end of the winter, when everyone is on edge, and provides the citizens with an opportunity to vent their spleens, disgorge their accumulated cabin-fevered frustrations and make general nuisances of themselves.

Late afternoon had brought clouds, cold and snow, which didn't reduce attendance at the meeting. Everyone had an axe to grind so they got there. Myrtle Fraser, the Methodist minister's wife, was a leading annual vocalist. She had a loud, uninformed, but definite opinion on every issue.

After unleashing a tirade against the Superintendent of Schools, who said the town couldn't afford a course in Bible study, Myrtle sat down. Next to her was a late arrival, Lew the Jew Pierce, clad in yellow Bermuda shorts, a many-striped shirt, a round, gaily tasseled cap and purple golf shoes. Slung over his shoulder was a bag of golf clubs. Lew reached into the bag, came out with a pint of Old Bantam, took a big pull, breathed a sigh of satisfaction and cheap whiskey at Myrtle Fraser and said: "Gawd, Myrtle, I thought I might hit a few but she's a snowin' too jeezly ha'hd."

Then, remembering his manners, Lew held the pint in front of Myrtle. "Shot?" he offered.

Having outraged the minister's wife with his ungodly behavior, Lew went on to an outstanding evening. Competent observers felt that possibly he'd surpassed his performance of 1927 when he'd attempted to kill the only three Democrats in town. In 1927 the Sheriff had booked him for "failure of attempted homicide" and let him go as soon as he sobered up. In 1959 the authorities were not as lenient and kept him in the county jail until his loving nephew, Dr. Pierce, bailed him out on Monday afternoon.

Hawkeye, over the weekend, devised a plan that included Lew the Jew for squeezing two hundred grand out of George Cogswell. He knew that George had the loot and that he had to give it to someone. A little hospital at Parsonsville, father down east, wanted the two hundred grand and had made an eloquent, superficially reasonable appeal. George really wanted to give the money to Parsonsville, but Hawkeye had shaken him when he said: "George, you'd be doing more for good medicine and for the public if you burned that joint in Parsonsville to the ground and found two young guys to go down there to practice and send their trouble to Spruce Harbor."

"Don't you think that rural areas deserve to have hospitals?" asked George.

"They deserve to have high-class combined nursing home-hospitals and facilities for the care of minor emergencies but, for the very sick, they should be no more than pit stops. Those guys practicing up in Parsonsville are nice guys but they don't know much. You give them two hundred grand and you put medical care in that area back twenty years."

"On the other hand," said George, "you want two hundred grand just so you can get a buddy down here to practice a way-out specialty."

"True. I don't deny that cardiac surgery is a wild idea for Spruce Harbor. Think a little, though. Trapper John is a smart guy who is a pro in a very fast league. We'll find work for him and the attention his act would bring to the hospital would attract money from other sources, like the goverment and the rich old broads who come here for the summer."

After springing his Uncle Lewis, still dressed for golf, from the county jail, Hawkeye stopped at a grocery and bought a cold six-pack, knowing that his relative would be a mite parched. "Have a brew, Jew," he said as soon as they'd passed the State Police barracks. "I hear you had a big night. Your uniform appears slightly rumpled."

"Son of a howah," Lew stated.

"Is that a brief, lucid, vivid, terse commentary on things in general, or do you have someone specifically in mind?" asked Hawkeye.

"Huh?" asked Lew, as he drained one can and reached for another.

"Look, Jew. I got an assignment for you. In a month or so I'm going to bring a guy over to Wawenock to play golf and I want you along and I want you to shoot no less than eighty-eight or more than ninety-two."

Lew, of course, wanted to know it all so Hawkeye gave his uncle some idea of what was going on. By the time they reached The Solid Rust Cadillac where a gaggle of cacophonous gulls greeted their master, Lew the Jew had committed himself, body and soul, to the establishment of a cardiovascular surgical department at Spruce Harbor General Hospital.

The next step was to line up Lucinda Lively. Hawkeye realized that this would require a delicate touch. Her participation might be necessary, or it might not be, but it would help. Lucinda, he knew, was happy in her present situation, but she very much wanted Trapper John to come to Spruce Harbor. George Cogswell, a tall, dark-haired, handsome bachelor, liked girls and Lucinda Lively liked men so Hawkeye hoped that he could blend all this into a useful public-spirited plan.

After office hours one day, Hawkeye asked Lucinda Lively: "How was your date with Trapper John the last time he was up? I've been meaning to ask but haven't had a chance."

Lucinda blushed. "What are you asking?"

"To be specific, I want to know how anxious you are to have him come to Spruce Harbor. I also want to know, quite specifically, if you'd try a little seduction on George Cogswell in order to get Trapper John to come to Spruce Harbor. I also want to know whether, if Trapper comes, you have an idea now, of whether you'd consider marrying him, sooner or later."

"Is that all you want to know?"

"Yeah. I guess that covers it."

Lucinda, the lovely blonde, cried. Hawkeye waited for the shower to pass. After a huge sob, she asked, "What makes you think Trapper would marry me?"

"Don't make me explain, but I know that if Trapper comes, it'll be partly because he wants you. He knows that you're the broad I've lined up for him and he knows how I feel about you so regardless of his big talk, he won't come unless he considers marriage a possibility. Obviously, neither of you would be committed but Trapper knows I'll clean his clock if he treats you like just another broad."

"He does, does he? So what's this about going to bed with George Cogswell?" Lucinda asked.

"I'm going to con George into a golf match with my uncle, Lew the Jew, and if George loses he's going to give us the two hundred grand Trapper needs to get in action. George can beat Lew, easy, so I'm arranging some distractions, one of which is you. I want you to caddy for him and I want him to think that if he loses you'll give him a roll in the hay. George is a pretty horny guy. I figure if you're there in the least clothing the weather allows, George may think too much to hit the ball."

Lucinda looked at Hawkeye as though he'd slapped her in the face. "You want me to be a howah?" wailed Lucinda.

"No, honey," said Hawkeye. "I'll keep you out of bed with George if you'll just go along with the idea. Think of what you'd be doing for the hospital and you know damn well that Trapper won't come without the two hundred grand. Of course you might catch Trapper even if he doesn't come here."

"I don't want him unless he comes here," said Lucinda.

In early May Hawkeye casually invited George Cogswell to the Wawenock Harbor Golf Course for a round of golf with Lew the Jew Pierce. The day was sunny, the south wind was warm, the fairways were drying out and George ate Wawenock alive. Seventy-two. Lew shot eighty-eight. Later George told Hawkeye that Lew the Jew's golf swing reminded him of Sugar Ray winding up for a bolo punch.

Over drinks at home in Crabapple Cove, Hawkeye said: "Hey, babe, you kind of clocked the Jew today. Do you think you could do it for two hundred grand?"

"I knew it. I just knew it, you son of a bitch. You're setting me up for something."

"It's very straightforward. I want a shot at the two hundred grand. I understand your position. But, will you give it a go? Eighteen holes, head to head, against Lew the Jew. If you win, Parsonsville gets the dough. If you lose, we get it for the cardiovascular unit and, to sweeten it, you get to spend the night with Lucinda Lively."

"What?" said George, nearly choking on his drink.

"Simple Lucinda's interested in you. I'm going to test your mettle. You handicap is if you win you lose a great piece of tail, at least for that night. After that, of course, you can make your own arrangements. George, I look upon this as a real character builder for you."

"Do you seriously think," asked George, "that I'd

blow a golf match and make a decision about two hundred grand just for a piece of tail?"

"I don't know," said Hawkeye, grinning, "but I want to find out."

George, who wouldn't have been employed by the Hamilton Foundation if he weren't a very straight arrow, was quite incensed at this proposition. "You know," he said, "I was thinking seriously of dumping Parsonsville, but you just made up my mind. Sure, I'll play Lew the Jew and I'm just likely to get the loser's bonus after I've won. Hawkeye, you're never going to see that two hundred grand."

"Okay if Doggy Moore and I play along with you and the Jew? Maybe give us a few blows, me and the Jew'll play you and Doggy a buck Nassau. Oh, did I tell you Lucinda's going to be your caddy?"

"Anything you say. Do we eat tonight or just drink?"

When the great day came George Cogswell showed up at Wawenock Harbor Golf Course full of confidence. He'd had a date, the night before, with Lucinda Lively, who had been very congenial.

Lucinda Lively, George's caddy, brought Little Eva, and explained that, should the usually accurate George stray, Eva would find his ball. Half A Man Timberlake, an experienced caddy, had been hired to work for Lew the Jew. Jocko Allcock, a prominent local sportsman, was Hawkeye's caddy and Doggy Moore rode his peculiarly equipped golf cart.

On the first tee Hawkeye Pierce watched Lucinda Lively, scantily clad in the shortest shorts and with just a token strip across her bosom, and, wondering if he could swing the club, was assailed, momentarily, by self-doubt. Never doubt, he told himself. Onward. Balls in the air. Hawkeye, Lew the Jew, Doggy Moore hit routine, safe drives on Wawenock's fairly easy first hole, a 340-yard par four from an elevated tee. George Cogswell teed up his ball, asked the half-naked Lucinda, who stayed closer than the average caddy, to ask Little Eva not to hang quite so close and topped his drive. He didn't complain, but he was aware that a flock of nearby seagulls had greeted the start of his swing with loud cries and squawks.

"You'd have made a great conductor," Hawk told his uncle, as they walked down the fairway.

"Ayuh," agreed Lew the Jew, who halved the hole with George Cogswell. On the second hole he showed the expertise which old-time Maine golfers knew about but which Goerge Cogswell hadn't seen. The second, a long, difficult dogleg to the right, called for two carefully placed shots if one hopes to be on in two. Lew the Jew's second shot was a four wood, which nestled in ten feet from the pin. George, hitting a seven iron, was ten yards short of the green. Just as the golfers and perhaps a dozen interested followers approached the green, all heard a shrill whistle. Out of nowhere a big gray seagull swooped down on Lew the Jew's ball, took it in his beak, flew toward the ocean and dropped the ball in a sand trap.

"By the Jesus," exclaimed Lew the Jew.

There was hurried consultation and everyone reached the same conclusion. You play them where they lie, and Lew's ball quite obviously lay in a sand trap to the right of the green.

"That ain't fayuh," commented Lew, who blasted out and two-putted, but George had chipped in close so his opponent was one down.

The third hole, a long par three, was halved when George missed a tricky four-footer for his par. As the group walked to the fourth tee, which had a densely wooded area behind it, Dr. Doggy Moore announced, "I got an appointment. I gotta sigmoidoscope Zeke

Simmons. I won't be long." Doggy drove his golf cart down the bumpy path behind the tee and soon the athletes and their entourage heard: "Goddamn it, Zeke, get your ass up on that rock and bend your legs up onto your chest. I told you if you couldn't get to the office, don't complain. I got a match to play. I ain't got all day."

On the tee, Little Eva stared balefully at George Cogswell who, one up and still confident, was annoyed that he'd missed a short putt but soothed by Lucinda Lively who hung close and exuded warmth and the promise of things to come. There was a sudden commotion behind the tee. Jocko Allcock appeared, half-leading, half-dragging Half A Man Timberlake, who was jumping up and down and saying over and over: "Me too. Me too!"

"What the hell's going on?" asked Hawkeye.

"No problem. Half A Man thinks he wants to get sigmoidoscoped but he'll be okay in a minute."

"Son of a howah," observed Lew the Jew.

The fourth is a par five, a long dogleg around a tidal inlet which at high tide is full of water and at low tide is a big mud flat. A drive to the right side of the fairway followed by anything from a five iron to a three wood across the inlet, depending on the wind, will get a good golfer home in two and set up an easy bird. George Cogswell put his drive in position and had only to decide whether to hit a three or four iron to the green. Lew the Jew, short off the tee, elected to play safe, so his second shot was calculated to set up a six or seven iron third shot.

Little Eva and Lucinda Lively watched their hero as he pondered the three or four iron. "Miss the shot, George," suggested Lucinda Lively. "I need you and I don't want to wait."

Before the match Lucinda Lively had told Hawkeye

she'd try to psyche George out of the match and if he lost she would have to depend on Hawkeye's promise. Therefore Hawkeye watched George's caddy on the fourth hole and his thought was that George, whether he went for a three or four iron, would be lucky to hit the ball. George did hit it, but it went into the drink.

"Oh, honey, I can't wait," said Lucinda Lively.

George and Lew the Jew halved five and six, and were still all even after eight holes, partly because the Jew was on top of his game and partly because Lucinda Lively and Little Eva distracted George just enough to keep Lew in contention. Hawkeye had debated whether to save operation amputation for the ninth or the eighteenth hole. Finding a group of slow-playing summer complaints on the ninth tee, Hawkeye quickly decided that now was the time to shake George Cogswell and provide the Jew with a one-up lead at the end of nine.

Hawkeye, the suave, engaging surgeon, approached the summer complaints, a pair of middle-aged married couples, explained that an important match was in progress and asked their permission to go through. Permission was granted gracefully. Just as George Cogswell went into his waggle and was about to start his backswing, there was a loud cry of "Help" from the left side of the narrow tree-lined fairway. Continuing to yell "Help," Wooden Leg Wilcox, who can go fairly quickly for a few yards, burst from the woods and started across the fairway, perhaps forty yards in front of the tee. Behind him, in hot pursuit, were Spearchucker Jones and his brother-in-law, a defensive tackle with the Forty-Niners, who was carrying a chain saw.

"What on earth is going on?" demanded a male summer complaint.

"Hard to tell," answered Hawkeye. "Five bucks

says the coons nail him before he gets to the other side of the fairway."

"Somebody do something," suggested George Cogswell.

"I don't believe we should interfere in a private quarrel. Of course, George, if you'd like to do something, go right ahead," Hawkeye said.

Within five yards of the woods to the right of the fairway, Wooden Leg Wilcox was caught by Spearchucker, who pinned him to the ground while his brother-in-law, to the tune of "Help, murder, save me," applied the chain saw to his right leg.

"My God, my God," wailed a female summer complaint, and echoed George's suggestion: "Somebody do something."

"Somebody be," Lew the Jew informed her. "Them two niggahs is sawin' that fella's leg off."

"Probably some sort of civil rights disagreement," said Hawkeye. "Shouldn't take long. Looks like a new chain saw."

"Now you mention it," Jocko Allcock chimed in, "we're pretty goddamn lucky 'round heah. Goddamn little racial tension."

"Call a doctor," screamed a female golfer.

"At your service, ma'am," offered Doggy Moore. "I'm a physician. In what way may I be of help?"

The female golfer fainted and Doggy took appropriate therapeutic measures while Spearchucker dragged his dismembered victim into the forest. His brother-in-law disdainfully threw the amputated leg into the woods, set the chain saw to rest on the edge of the fairway, and approached the golfers.

"Awfully sorry if we disturbed your game," he said apologetically. "I play myself and I realize that this sort of thing may be upsetting. Hope we didn't hold you up too long."

"Perfectly all right," said Hawkeye. "I presume you know what you're doing, but there is one thing. If this ever happens again, I hope you'll have your victim yell 'fore,' rather than 'help' or 'murder.' Whether you realize it or not, there are very strict rules of etiquette on the golf course, and in my opinion you have broken several of them. Were you a member. I would bring you before the grievance committee."

"I'm very sorry, sir," said the defensive tackle, who departed with a hangdog air.

"Now," said Hawkeye, "I hope that satisfies everyone. You heard me tell him where to head in. Hit the ball, George."

George barely hit it for the next two holes, but he managed to win the eleventh and twelfth, pulling even again with Lew the Jew. When they'd played the fourth hole the first time around Doggy'd done a sigmoidoscopy and the cove had been half full of water. Now the tide was gone and Lew, instead of aiming down the fairway, took dead aim at the green, two hundred and fifty yards of fairway, bushes and mud flats from the tee.

"Great Baldheaded, Unrevised, North American Protestant Jesus Christ! What's that foolish bastard figurin' to do?" asked Jocko quietly.

"He's trying to hit that sand bar in the middle of the cove. It's not out of bounds, and he could get on from there with a wedge. I've seen him do it before."

Lew the Jew hit the ball a ton, maybe a hundred and eighty yards, and whistled as the ball landed on the elevated ridge of sand. The big gray gull swooped down, picked it up, flew to the green and dropped it two feet from the cup.

"Son of a howah!" said Lew the Jew.

"Great drive, Jew," said Hawkeye. "I never seen you so long off the tee."

George Cogswell stood on the tee, gulping like a frog. He knew from here on in he didn't have a chance.

"Okay," said George. "I'm not stupid. I'm tired of golf. Hawk, you got the two hundred grand. Lucinda and I have some business, don't we, honey?"

"Oh, yes, George, Let's get it going."

As George, Lucinda and Little Eva left for the clubhouse, Hawkeye said to his uncle, "I hadn't anticipated such a sudden conclusion. That Jewish duck of yours has a lot of talent."

"By Jesus, Hawk," said his uncle, "they got a nice '49 Caddy in to Strong's garage for only four hundred dollar. You know I been thinkin' of gittin' me a mobile home and givin' the Solid Rust Cadillac to the gulls."

"Go get it, Jew," said his nephew. "I'm buying."

Before the golf game, Hawkeye had given Lucinda a large black capsule and said, "After the match, George will probably take you to the Spruce Harbor Motel for drinks and dinner. Swallow this before your first drink and don't have over three."

The next morning George Cogswell stopped at the hospital to see Hawkeye.

"How was it, George?" asked Hawk. "Pretty good?"

"Lucinda Lively has the wrong name," said George. "Her name should be Sleeping Beauty, and you, Pierce, are a low-down, cheating fornicator of swine."

8

Hawkeye Pierce had no interest in contributing to the morass of medical literature, to what he called the Journals of Unnecessary Research. But, now and then, he spent three consecutive nights writing about a case that interested, helped or hurt him. He wrote for fun, to reinforce his psyche, or to escape the reality of people dying of cancer, maybe somehow to find some sense in it, somewhere.

The *Maine Medical Journal,* like all minor and most major medical journals, is devoted to distillations of other medical writing, cloudy, meaningless investigations of subjects discussed clearly elsewhere or scientifically suspect analyses of rare cases. Therefore, Hawkeye was not surprised to get a letter from Hank Manley, Secretary of the Maine State Medical Society and Editor of the *Maine Medical Journal,* asking if Hawkeye would be interested in doing a paper on cancer of the trachea or windpipe.

One week later Hawkeye wrote Hank Manley a note and sent a story with it. The note said:

Dear Hank:

If there are two cases a year of carcinoma of the trachea in the State of Maine, I'd be surprised. So, I don't think a "paper" on this subject would be a major contribution. However, I just happen to have had a case of carcinoma of the trachea. What I've written ain't a paper. It's the story of Moose Lord. What little there is to know about carcinoma of the trachea you can look up, and good luck to you. I don't expect you to print the story of Moose Lord in the *Maine Medical Journal,* nor would I want you to, but I thought you might like to read it. Here it is.

THE SOUND OF THE MOOSE

Everyone who's lobstered in Muscongus Bay in the last thirty-five years has heard the Sound of the Moose. On still, foggy mornings out in the bay the silence is punctuated by a variety of familiar sounds: the cry of seagulls; the murmur of surf as gentle morning swells meet rocky island shores; the whack-whack of make-and-break engines in lobster boats; and, when I was a boy, the Sound of the Moose, which came rolling across the water and through the fog like a voice from another world. It was a deep, booming, but lulling call, a welcome, happy, comforting sound. If one listened carefully, he could make out the words:

Yes, we'll gather at the river,
The beautiful, the beautiful river,
Gather with the saints at the river
That flows by the throne of God.

When my father Big Benjy Pierce and I heard it, we'd pause for a moment, smile and go back to work. Sometimes the old man would say, "The Sound of the Moose is heard on the sea," and usually add, "I wish Moose would pay more attention to lobsterin' and less to hymn singin'."

The Moose was Jonas Lord. Jonas lived in a one-room shack on Indian Island on the south side of Crabapple Cove. Only at high tide is it a real island. At low tide a reef of mud and rock connects it to the mainland. When I visited Jonas as a kid, I walked, swam or rowed Big Benjy's skiff, depending on the tide, the time of year or the mood I was in. Jonas was a big, tall, bull-necked guy with wide sloping shoulders. He had an expressive, happy face, which reflected humor, kindness, understanding and love for everything. Sometimes confusion and blankness seemed to take over but never for long. The physical sum of Jonas Lord was a man who had to be nicknamed Moose. Moose particularly loved kids, and all kids loved him.

The Moose lobstered and clammed. He read the Bible, but not too well. He couldn't read anything too well. He played the fiddle and sang at Saturday-night dances. He sang in his shack on Indian Island and in his lobster boat and in church every Sunday. Some of his scant income was spent on food and some on gasoline for his boat. The little left over was spent on kids. For five years he bought me a book every month.

Thinking back, I can't be sure that Jonas Lord thought any more of me than he did of the others, but I hung around him more and required more of him. He taught me secrets of lobstering and clamming that some people in the business still don't know. I sat in his shack for hours while he carved ship models and told me stories of the sea and Crabapple Cove. When I graduated from high school he gave me a model of a clipper ship. As I sit here and write I can look up and see it on my mantelpiece.

Martha Hobbs came to teach in Crabapple Cove's one-room, eight-grade schoolhouse while I was in Port Waldo High. Martha was tall, pretty and smart. She liked to dance and in those days, particularly during the summer, there was a dance somewhere at least two nights a week. Everyone wanted to dance with Martha. Jonas Lord was always in the two-, three- or four-man band playing his fiddle. When Martha danced, Moose followed her every move with his big, gentle, vacant, twinkling eyes.

The Moose was the Moose and he lived in his shack on Indian Island and he was there because he was supposed to be there. He was a special gift to the children of Crabapple Cove. Any change in status was unthinkable. But time changes things, even in Crabapple Cove.

One day in May of my freshman year at Androscoggin College, Big Benjy appeared at the fraternity house demanding to see me. He'd come to bring me home because the Moose and Martha Hobbs were getting married in the Cove church that night. Benjy was going to be best man, and I was to be an usher and hand out the refreshments afterward.

I remember that wedding as though it were yesterday. The altar with candles burning. My old man in a black suit resurrected from heaven knows where. The guests, some of them in rubber boots. The Moose, with his happy smile and his eyes like saucers as he looked in wonder at his bride. Martha, happy, proud, sure she had the man she wanted.

Jonas, Jr. appeared a year or so later and was followed by four more children in the next decade. I was in college, medical school, internship, surgical residency or the army during and after this period. My visits home were infrequent, but I never hit the Cove without calling on Moose, Martha and their kids. They still lived on Indian Island. Three more rooms were tacked on to the original shack. The children were blond, bright, and well-behaved. They called me Uncle

Hawkeye or Dr. Hawkeye. That's my name hereabouts because the only book Big Benjy read before I was born, or since, was *The Last of the Mohicans.*

Eventually I became the chest surgeon at Spruce Harbor and built a new house near my parents' farm in Crabapple Cove. I'd always wanted to come home to live, but there was something I had overlooked. People in the Cove are geared to a certain pace and economy. Inevitably, I had become geared to another style of life. Nobody in the Cove except me is ever in a hurry. I salute old friends with a preoccupied wave when, by local custom, I should stop and pass the time of day.

When I first came home I called on Moose and Martha occasionally, but the visits dwindled as I got busier. By May of last year I hadn't seen the Moose to talk to for six months although I'd occasionally passed him on the road and waved. Big Benjy mentioned in April that Jonas wasn't feeling well. I said, "Well, tell him to see one of the local doctors, and if it's anything in my line, he can come over to the hospital."

A few weeks later I got a message to call Dr. Ralph Young in Port Waldo, who said, "Hawkeye, I want you to see the Moose. Can I send him right up?"

"What's wrong with him?"

"He can't breathe."

"Send him. I'll be here."

I happened to be looking out a window an hour later when Moose, Martha and Jonas, Jr. pulled up in front of the Spruce Harbor General Hospital in their old rattletrap. Moose's big shoulders were slumped. His walk was unsteady. Martha and young Jonas helped him. I thought to myself: whatever it is, it isn't good.

As I walked toward the entrance I had a clear realization: here is a guy who's practically been a second father. I live within a mile of him. I've known he's been sick and I haven't been to see him in six months.

Finding a wheelchair, I met them at the door. Moose grinned at me. His eyes twinkled. He put his arms around me and gave me a hug. He sat down in the chair and asked, "How they goin', Hawkeye?" The Sound of the Moose had changed. It was a husky, croaking voice, hardly a voice at all.

I saw the lump in his neck. This, the stertorous breathing and the hoarseness meant trouble. I make my living from tragedy. I try do do my best and view it philosophically. I can't allow emotion to interfere with surgical thinking or performance, but when I heard the Moose's voice and felt the lump in his neck I had a moment of panic.

I wheeled him to the operating room and announced that I wanted to look into his windpipe and bronchial tubes under local anesthesia. The diagnosis was easy. A biopsy showed he had carcinoma of the windpipe, with spread of the cancer to the right side of his neck.

One can practice thoracic surgery for a lifetime and never see a carcinoma of the trachea. I had to find one in Moose Lord. After the bronchoscopy I wandered aimlessly for a few minutes. Moose, Martha and their oldest boy were in my office waiting for the word. I entered, sat down and said, "Moose, how long has this been going on?"

"A year or so, Hawkeye."

"Why didn't you let me know?"

"Didn't think nawthin' of it at first."

"Why didn't you go to a doctor?"

"I did a couple months ago. He gimme some medicine, but it didn't help me none."

The Moose kept right on having a smile on his big

face and a twinkle, or something, in his large, confused eyes.

I tapped my knuckles on the desk, summoning courage, and finally I said, "Moose, you're in trouble. You have cancer of your windpipe and it's already spread to your neck. It is unlikely that anything can be done about it. If anybody can do anything, it's going to involve extensive surgery with little chance of a cure."

The grin drooped a little and the twinkle lost some of its glint. I looked at Martha. She was looking at Jonas.

Moose, in his croaking voice, said, "Take a crack at her, Hawk. Ain't nobody goin' to blame you if she don't work out."

"This is a rare kind of cancer, Moose. No one has much experience with it. I have none. You'd be better off in Boston where a few people know something about it. You'll need X-ray treatments, too. In Boston they have X-ray equipment we don't have."

"I want you, Hawkeye."

"Moose, I'm going to admit you to the hospital. You and Martha talk it over. I think you oughta go to Boston or maybe New York."

After Jonas was admitted I headed for Crabapple Cove, driving too fast, like a little boy scurrying home to where it's safe. Crabapple Cove was always safe for little boys because Moose Lord was there. But now he wasn't there. I went directly to my parents' house. Stalking into the kitchen and shoving aside nieces and nephews, I identified one of the assembled multitude as a younger brother.

"Where's the old man?" I demanded.

"Around."

"Find him!"

Big Benjy was summoned from the barn. "Gawd,"

he said, "it's Hawkeye." Leaving the kitchen, he yelled to my mother, "Woman, put on your best dress! A famous surgeon has come to visit us."

I have to take a certain amount of guff from Benjy. He is my senior by only nineteen years and he's never been out of shape.

"Dad, I want to talk to you and Mother."

He moved the crowd out, and Mother joined us.

"What's the trouble, Hawk?" my father asked.

"It's the Moose. He has cancer of the windpipe. Barring an act of God, he's going to die, soon and hard."

Mother broke the silence. "Can't you help him, Hawkeye?"

"I doubt it, Ma."

"He's had trouble for a long time. I told you about it," said Benjy.

"I know, but if he was in trouble why didn't he come to me?"

"You've gotten to be a pretty hard man to find, boy. People around here don't feel free to come to you."

"People around here don't get the idea, but Jonas Lord should know better."

"Maybe us folks in Crabapple Cove figure you've lost track of us a little," Benjy said, "but don't blame yourself for the Moose. Martha and me and your mother have been after him. He wouldn't come to you back along. He knew he was in trouble, but he wouldn't face it. Now he's so sick he has to, and I know you'll do your best for him."

I drove home, mixed a drink, went into the study and thought. I consulted my surgical journals and read everything of significance that had been printed about carcinoma of the trachea in the last five years. It didn't take long because not much had been written.

Mary brought in a cold lobster, a pot of coffee and

didn't ask questions. After finishing the reading, the lobster and the coffee, I called Maxie Neville in New York.

His secretary answered: "Who's calling, please?"

"Omit the evasive technique and lemme talk to the boss."

"It's the clamdigger," I heard her say.

The famous surgeon came to the phone. "Hi, boy. How are things in the boondocks?"

"I need help," I said.

"Okay. Tell me."

"What do you do for carcinoma of the trachea?"

After a brief pause the answer came: "You unload it. You can't win. It's grief. There isn't much more to say."

"My very own thoughts. Will you take it?"

"If you want me to. Tell me more."

"Max, you remember Moose Lord, whom we visited when you came to Crabapple Cove? The guy on the island? He's the patient."

Another pause: "Boy, you really are in trouble. Play it any way you like, but I'll tell you something."

"What?"

"You're stuck with this one. Moose won't want to go to Boston or New York or to any other surgeon. It would take a miracle to fix him, and in this kind of deal you have as good a chance as anyone else."

He went on to give me a few suggestions. When he was through I'd accepted the fact that it had to be me and the Moose, all the way.

Martha Lord arrived.

"Jonas and I have talked it over, Hawkeye," she said. "He doesn't want to go away. He wants you to take care of him."

She looked as though she were going to cry. I hoped she wouldn't.

"I'll do my best for him, Martha," I said, "but it won't be good enough."

"Hawkeye, I know you'll do your best."

Martha and Mary started on coffee while I wandered into the warm moonlit spring night. There's a creek about fifty yards behind my house, and May is the month when smelts run up the tidal creeks. I walked down to see if they were running, but the tide was too low, so I lay on the bank, looked at the moon and thought like a surgeon and made some plans. We'd do a right radical neck dissection, remove the larynx and as much of the trachea as we had to. Win or lose, we'd give it a go.

The next day I discussed the case with Joe Berry, the new ear, nose and throat man, who agreed to help. Me Lay Marston and his anesthesia service threw in a few good ideas. The blood bank was alerted to the probability of great need and Moose was put on the schedule for Monday morning.

I sat down with Moose and told him what to expect. While I talked he looked at me and smiled his bland smile. The big eyes were inscrutable. I couldn't read them and didn't want to.

Talking was an effort. He put his big arm around my shoulder, gasped for air and croaked, "Don't you worry none, Hawkeye."

I left quickly, half in panic again. Here was the Moose telling *me* not to worry. I was sure he knew he'd had the course. He would let me chop him up if it would give him a little more time to watch his kids grow and because everybody would be unhappy if he just went ahead and died.

The interval before the operation demonstrated clearly that Jonas Lord was an important man in my part of the world. He had no money and few material assets, but he certainly had friends. Usually the interest people show in someone else's operation is morbid curiosity. Secretly they are hoping for the worst. Not so this time. Few asked questions. They smiled and waved. The password seemed to be: Good luck on Monday.

On Sunday I played golf and went to a clambake afterward without having a very good time. I had the butterflies, like before a football game. In the evening I read more articles on carcinoma of the trachea and went to bed early.

I usually eat breakfast at Wink's Diner in Port Waldo. Wink's early-morning customers nearly always include people I went to school with, played ball with or ran around with at some time in the past. As a rule, breakfast is accompanied by good-natured banter, betting on ball games, and so forth.

When I entered Wink's on my way to operate on the Moose, no one said more than "good morning." A few nodded and smiled. I ate ham and eggs and perused the sports section of the paper. The Sox had dropped a double-header. Vaguely I wished that time had not run out on Theodore Samuel Williams. The waitress was my cousin Eunice Pierce. Cousin Eunice and I have never been very close, but she is not so poorly acquainted as to call me "Doctor." When I paid my check, however, she said, "Good luck today, Doctor." Walking toward the door, I was halted by a familiar voice saying, "Hey, Hawkeye."

It was an old and good friend. "We'll all be praying for the Moose and you today," he said and turned quickly back to his coffee.

On the way to Spruce Harbor I decided that this was an unusual situation. People were thinking of the patient, and they were thinking of the doctor, too. I was glad they were. Other thoughts drifted into my mind. I remembered the Moose and my old man yelling at me during football games. I remembered the only time Moose ever left the State of Maine. He and Big Benjy rode a truckful of lobsters to New York to see me graduate from medical school.

Halfway to Spruce Harbor I almost aimed the car for Canada, but I didn't. I settled down. The butterflies drowned in my stomach and my brain started to function.

We had quite a morning. Early in the operation we discovered that the cancer was even more extensive than we'd thought.

"You've had it, Hawkeye. We'd better quit," advised Joe Berry.

"Not today. Today I'm swinging for the fences. I'm going to get this thing out or cool him trying. I'm not going to send him back to the ward and watch him choke to death. At least, I don't want to."

When we'd finished, most of the trachea had been removed, the larynx was out and the right side of the neck had been dissected. The Moose's blood pressure and pulse never wavered. He'd had four pints of blood. There was no visible or palpable cancer left behind.

Leaving the operating room after five hours of hard labor I was limp and unrealistically optimistic. I'd been in the business too long to think I was God's gift to surgery. I knew perfectly well the thing had to show up again somewhere. Still, once in a blue moon you get real lucky and a wild hope began to grab me. Maybe we had a win. At the very least, Moose would be able to breathe and he would be around a while longer. A reprieve is better than nothing. I felt like I'd pitched a no-hitter in the World Series.

By evening Moose was awake. He looked at me and

gave me his big damn foolish grin again. "We did it, Moose," I said. "You're gonna be home in two weeks." His eyes laughed at me.

I talked to Martha and young Jonas. We had a temporary victory, I told them. How long it would last was impossible to know. Statistically the chance of permanent cure was slight.

Moose was in unbelievably good shape the next day. He even got out of bed and walked. For the first time in months he could breathe freely and easily, but the first of many problems presented itself. Moose could no longer talk because I'd removed his talking equipment. Usually such a patient communicates by writing notes until he learns esophageal speech. Writing was out for the Moose because his writing was worse than his reading. He could scribble notes, but I couldn't read them. I brought in people who had learned esophageal speech. They tried to teach him and he made progress, but not much.

Otherwise he did well. I got the impression that he wasn't fond of his present situation and figured it was too good to last, if that makes sense. At least he was breathing, eating and walking, which was more than he could do before surgery.

Two weeks after surgery, Moose and I left the hospital together and headed for Crabapple Cove. There is a system of communication around the Cove which I've never understood. Everyone knew Moose was coming home. To say that the streets were crowded with well-wishers would be an exaggeration because there are no streets and the houses are three hundred yards apart, even where they're bunched in together. Nevertheless, a group waited in front of each house to say hello to Moose, and I had to stop. He shook hands and smiled at everybody. I met more of my neighbors than I had in years. The tide was high when we reached the shore opposite Indian Island. Young Jonas met us in the lobster boat and took his father home.

The magic held through the summer. Moose gained strength, even learned to talk again in a crude sort of way and hauled a few lobsters. The smile never left, nor did it regain its former radiance. The time was borrowed and Moose seemed to know it. I knew it but hoped anyhow. Whenever I could I went to see him. Sometimes I told him the stories he'd told me twenty-five years before. His eyes would light up and the grin almost made a comeback. Occasionally, when the tide was high in the evening, Moose and I and our kids would dangle lines off the rocks and catch tom cod and cunners. Despite my concern for him I had a good summer, and, I hope, so did he.

I kept thinking he should have a neck dissection on the left side. Every time I saw him I felt his neck. In early October the lump appeared.

He knew it was there.

"We gotta stick the knife to you again, Moose," I told him.

He sucked in wind and tried to make words. They came out spasmodically. "The hell with it."

"I know how you feel, Moose, but we're going right down the line. We're in too deep to back out now."

A week later Joe Berry and I set out to do a left radical neck dissection. Before we started I examined the right side of his neck where we'd operated previously. There was a lump that I hadn't felt before. A biopsy confirmed the obvious. There was recurrent cancer on the right side.

We were licked. I sent Moose home to ride it out as best he could. I decided, for a while, to forego X-ray treatment. I wanted him to be home as long as possible.

In November an epidemic of flu struck Crabapple Cove. Moose caught it, coughed, wheezed and became short of breath. I gave him this and that, none of which helped. He began to form crusts in his tracheostomy, where we'd sewed the short stump of windpipe to the skin—where he breathed. Too many crusts, too little air.

I carry a bronchoscope in my car. Two or three nights a week I'd go to Indian Island, find Moose struggling for air, stick the scope down and pull out the crusts. He'd breathe clearly then, look at me gratefully, grin a little and shake his head. Three days before Thanksgiving he almost suffocated before I arrived. I pulled out another big crust and insisted that he return to the hospital. On Thanksgiving morning I cleaned out his windpipe as thoroughly as possible before taking him home to Indian Island for the day. He didn't eat much turkey. The lumps in his neck were getting bigger and swallowing was difficult.

The next morning I picked up Moose on the shore opposite Indian Island. Before he boarded the car for Spruce Harbor, he stood for a moment and looked. He looked at his island and then out across the bay. He looked at all the little islands and the places where the lobsters live. The last look. We both knew it.

From there on Moose did it the hard way. The cancer in his neck got larger. X-ray treatments were no help. New drugs which halt some cancers did nothing to this one. The crusts kept forming in his remaining stump of windpipe, despite fog tents and anything else I could think of. Jonas became more and more confused. He'd get out of the fog tent. He'd manage to mess up anything that might help to keep his airway open. Fortunately he had only a few moments of real awareness.

I put him in a private room and left a bronchoscope at the bedside along with forceps to pull out the crusts. Sometimes, between us, Joe Berry and I scoped him five or six times a day. Once, after I cleaned him out, Moose woke up and looked at me. No sound came, but his lips made the words: "Let me go, Hawk."

"I'd like to, Moose, but I can't," was my painful, stupid answer.

As Christmas approached there was slow but definite improvement. The crusts didn't form as often. Jonas had longer periods of consciousness. I spent as much time with him as I could. The only question he asked, or tried to ask, was, "When is Christmas?"

It was ten days, then five days, and finally one day until Christmas. Before I went home that afternoon, Moose issued his daily statement. With a smile, he gulped and grunted, "I'm going to make it to Christmas!"

We trimmed our tree on Christmas Eve and put the kids to bed. Mary and I had presents for Moose's family. So did Mother and Big Benjy. At nine o'clock Benjy arrived in his boat and we went to Indian Island. Somehow, Martha and her children were managing to achieve a very real, if subdued, feeling of happiness and thankfulness on Christmas Eve.

Big Benjy and I stayed a while, had coffee, left our presents and took off. I got up at five o'clock Christmas morning so that I could go to Spruce Harbor, see Moose and get back in time to open presents. When I entered the hospital, the night supervisor said, "Good morning, Dr. Pierce. Mr. Lord is wide awake and waiting for you."

I hurried to his room and found Moose sitting on the side of the bed. He gave me a grin reminiscent of better days. He indicated that I should sit down beside him. He was alert, breathing clearly and talking better than he had in two months.

"Merry Christmas, Hawk."

"Same to you, Moose."

"The family's coming up after church."

"I know it, Moose. Benjy and I were out to the island last night."

"Hawk, it won't be much longer."

I started to say something or other. He put his big hand on my shoulder.

"Don't kid me, Hawk. I'm happy. I don't mind. I've had a good life."

All this with grunts and gasps or just movements of his lips, but with the smile shining through as it hadn't for so long.

"Okay, Moose." All I could do was put my arm around him.

"Hawkeye, will you keep an eye on Martha and the kids?"

"Moose, you know it."

His smile got bigger. "You go home to your family, Hawk."

"I'll see you tomorrow, Moose."

The eyes laughed at me again. He shook his head. "Good-bye, Hawk. You been a good friend," he whispered, holding out his hand.

I shook hands, said, "So long, Moose," and started to go. I turned, went back and sat beside him again.

"Moose," I said, "have a good trip. Before you leave, I ought to say something about how much you've meant to me, but you know it, so I don't have to."

His arm, no longer big and strong, circled my shoulder and gave me a squeeze.

"Go home, Hawk," said the silent lips.

Toward the end of the ride home I achieved a degree of tranquillity. We'd fought a good fight. Moose was happy. He was going to enjoy Christmas. I'd try to.

After the presents were opened, Mary and the kids

went to the Crabapple Cove Church. They didn't invite me, but after they left I decided to go too. I joined my family in the back row. The stares of the congregation reminded me that the last time I was in church was when Moose Lord married Martha Hobbs. Three rows in front of me and my family sat Martha Lord and her five children.

The phone beside my bed rang at three A.M. on the day after Christmas.

"Dr. Pierce."

"Yes."

"Mr. Lord has just expired."

"Thank you."

I dressed and looked out the window. The tide was high. I drove to my parents' house and banged on the door.

Big Benjy appeared.

"Moose?" he asked.

"Yeah. How about taking me out to the island?"

The temperature was three above. The moon was full, and the night was clear. The lobster boat crashed through a skim of ice around the dock and in a few minutes we were at Indian Island.

Martha and her children heard our motor and met us at the dock.

"Martha, Jonas died an hour ago."

She paused a moment before saying, "Thank you, Hawkeye. Thank you so much for everything. You and Benjy come in and have some coffee."

"I don't want no coffee," my old man growled. "Martha, what do you want us to do? You tell us, we'll do it."

"Everything's taken care of for now, Benjy," she assured him. "We'll need some help in the next few days, and we'll let you know."

"Thanks, Hawkeye," said Jonas, Jr.

Big Benjy and I got back in the boat. There wasn't a breath of wind, and the bay was bathed in moonlight. Only our motor broke the silence as Benjy headed for the open sea.

"Where you going?" I asked.

"Nowhere."

About half a mile out he cut the motor and opened a pint of Old Bantam whiskey. We drifted. I identified Wreck Island a little way south. We didn't talk, just nipped at the pint and smoked.

After a while I thought I heard something. Big Benjy perked up his ears. He'd heard it too, and looked kind of scared.

I climbed out of the cabin and looked down a beam of moonlight which made a path from the boat right back to Indian Island. At the end of the moonbeam I saw Martha and her children standing on the rocks in front of their house. They were singing Moose Lord's favorite hymn:

> Yes, we'll gather at the river,
> The beautiful, the beautiful river,
> Gather with the saints at the river
> That flows by the throne of God.

Quietly, slowly, reverently, Big Benjy Pierce said, "Boy, everything's all right. The Sound of the Moose is still heard on the sea."

9

Four months before the opening of the clinic and the completion of the new Spruce Harbor General, Trapper John McIntyre arrived. He had left the city forever and would, he said, devote himself to supervising the construction and outfitting of the cardiovascular unit.

Three days after Trapper's arrival Lucinda Lively, Dr. Pierce's secretary, submitted her resignation.

"Trapper works fast, I guess," said Hawkeye with an attempt at cheerfulness.

"I like him a lot and I'm going to be with him and work for him and have fun."

"*Vaya con Dios,* babe. Trapper got a place to live?"

"Oh yes," chirped Lucinda. "We're going to live in a tent on Thief Island."

"That should be fun for the summer," said Hawkeye. "You'll be sort of tented up, I take it."

"Oh, very funny. And it's not just for the summer. Trapper says he's going to get a stove like you guys had in Korea and a wooden floor and something to cook on and a refrigerator and this and that and we're going to live there the year around."

"Just like that?"

"Just like that, Dr. Pierce," said Lucinda, who kissed him and walked out without looking back.

Hawkeye Pierce had been working hard and it would take a while to find a new secretary so he declared himself on vacation. He left word that Trapper John would cover him for necessary chest surgery and that he was going to spend a month at home, on the golf course and on his boat.

Two weeks into vacation, Hawkeye heard that Trapper was growing a beard and frequently appeared at the hospital barefoot and clad only in the briefest of swimming trunks. Furthermore, the word was that Trapper's companion, Lucinda Lively, now wore only a bikini.

One morning Sue Taylor, the OR supervisor, called Dr. Pierce's home and proclaimed, "You've gotta do something about that boy of yours. I won't have him coming into my OR in swimming trunks and I won't have him training that floozy as a scrub nurse, either."

"Sue, baby," purred Hawkeye, "you haven't been watching the scoreboard. It's not your OR anymore. Duke, Trapper, Spearchucker and Hawkeye have bought you out. We got it going for us so you and everybody else are going to play our rules. It doesn't matter how Trapper dresses. All that matters is how he works and if he wants to train Lucinda as a scrub nurse it's none of your goddamn business."

"I'll resign," proclaimed Sue.

"No, you won't. Why don't you get a bikini? If you look good in it, I'll give you a try."

"You're disgusting. He smells like a haddock. That damn fool Wooden Leg is teaching him to fillet fish. He could at least wash the scales off before he comes to the hospital."

"I think you may have a point there, Sue. You tell Trapper I say to take a shower before doing surgery, or I'll burn down his tent."

Sue Taylor had the bit in her teeth. An impulsive, determined, capable, well-meaning, somewhat unexposed forty-year-old product of Tedium Cove, she could not cope easily with change. "Do you know what Dr. McIntyre and that blond are doing when they're not working or cutting fish or making love in that little cranberry patch on Thief Island?" she asked, continued and persisted.

"No. What?"

"They're peddling fish. Wooden Leg bought a new truck and they're going around to all the summer places. Leg says everybody wants to get a look at them and to look at them they gotta buy fish. He thinks maybe you oughta get a new heart surgeon and let Trapper just peddle fish."

"What's this about the cranberry patch?"

"You'll hear about it," said Sue. "I'm not one to gossip."

"Of course," said Hawkeye. "Relax, babe. Everything'll be okay." He knew of Thief Island's cranberry patch, guessed what was happening there and grinned.

Fog in June on the coast of Maine is as inevitable as the tasteless lumps of batter called fried clams in a hundred greasy spoons along U.S. Route 1. Fog is here, it's there, it's everywhere. The Flying Passage between Hungry Island and Long Island may be socked in like black bean soup while the sun sheds its morning glory on everything three hundred yards to the east or west. At six A.M. on the morning of June 10, Wrong Way Napolitano, the Italian kamikaze pilot, the owner and only pilot of the Spruce Harbor and Inter-Island Air Service, arrived at his hangar. Mr. Napolitano made wrong moves, now and then, but he usually could find his hangar, which was small, unobtrusive and well away from the action at Spruce Harbor International Airport. The airport acquired its international designation two weeks after the glorious day when an Icelandic Airways DC-3 on a flight from Copenhagen via Reykjavik to New York landed and disgorged a mother who had not expected a premature Viking.

Wrong Way Napolitano started the Spruce Harbor and Inter-Island Air Service in 1953. This was just after his discharge from the air force, which, having discovered several of his major problems, had made him a flying instructor. Wrong Way had visions of glory like an earlier Maine hero, Miniver Cheevy of Tilbury Town, almost fifty miles away, who'd dreamt of Thebes and Camelot and Priam's neighbors. Wrong Way had never heard of Miniver Cheevy, but he had read somewhere of Qantas, the Australian airline, which started as the Queensland and Northern Territories Air Service. Wrong Way, as he flew over Penobscot Bay spotting schools of fish for his brothers, uncles and cousins, dreamed of the Spruce Harbor and Inter-Island Air Service becoming an international airline with lots of big jets. But he could never figure out how to pronounce SHAIIAS, so he just dreamed.

Wrong Way Napolitano, long before this sunny, foggy morning, had earned his name and fame as an Italian kamikaze pilot for three quite good reasons. One: he was Italian, two: he often flew in the wrong direction, and three: he was even money to run into something. Such as the Eagle Head Lighthouse, the Pemaquid Point Lighthouse, the mast on *The Maria and Luigi*, a well-known gillnetter owned by Maria and Luigi, and the steeple of the Spruce Harbor Congregational Church.

The fact that Wrong Way Napolitano was still alive intrigued many observers but could be explained with clarity and insight by Wooden Leg Wilcox who, when asked for his opinion, said: "The dumb guinea can't hit anything square."

Wrong Way, in rebuttal, declared that his precarious longevity was owing to "a great set of reflexes." This declaration was usually made in the Bay View Café and united the customers in a feeling of togetherness which no other declaration, on any subject, by any man, could bring to pass. As one voice, they chorused: "Bullshit."

At six o'clock on the morning of June 10 the Spruce Harbor International Airport was shrouded in fog. Whether Wrong Way knew this or not was questionable but, undaunted, he took off in his new Piper Tri-Pacer and, finding the sun, flew toward it and, as luck would have it, found himself where he was supposed to be. Below him he saw Matinicus Island and the early-morning blue-green calm of Penobscot Bay. Left behind was the fog which obscured the mainland. He proceeded, from a thousand feet up, to look for schools of fish. The idea was that, if he saw any, he would report their whereabouts by radio to his relatives in the trawlers below.

By nine fifteen the fog had redistributed itself so that Wrong Way could see neither schools of fish nor Matinicus Island. An uncle on the radio said: "Time to go home, Wrong Way. Which way you headin' in?"

"Guess I'll aim her for Eagle Head Light and from there I can pick my way in over Thief Island."

"Finestkind, Wrong Way," said the voice on the radio. "We know you can find the light. The question is can you get past it?"

"Go to hell," replied Wrong Way. "Over."

Another voice chimed in: "Hey, Wrong Way, if you don't run into Eagle Head Light within seven minutes, keep your eyes peeled for the Eiffel Tower."

Wrong Way Napolitano uttered a crude suggestion and headed for home. At this approximate time, on Thief Island, Trapper John McIntyre and Lucinda Lively finished breakfast and luxuriated in the warmth of the sun, which had begun to penetrate the fog. On all sides there was gloom, but Thief Island was blessed with an ethereal sunlit haze which, like almost everything, turned the highly suggestible mind of Trapper John to thoughts of love. He and Lucinda had discovered a tiny cranberry bog in one corner of the island's central clearing. In June a cranberry bog is no good for cranberries, but when a blanket is placed upon it it does provide a soft, secluded area in which to express one's most tender sentiments.

Trapper John preferred indirection in these matters, so instead of saying. "Let's go over to the cranberry patch and get laid," he said, "How about a swim?"

Lucinda countered with: "Cranberry patch first, hon. Then a swim."

Fifteen seconds before consummating their most tender sentiments, the lovers heard a sound which became a noise and then an all-consuming roar. Wrong Way Napolitano, flying at fifty feet, spotted Thief Island, breathed a deep sigh of relief, skimmed the treetops on the south shore, looked down, saw the action in the cranberry bog and reacted instinctively. Wrong Way's instinct often takes over when the call is for judgment. In this case, one must suppose that he instinctively wanted to participate rather than watch. Convulsively, he pushed forward on the controls, took dead aim for the cranberry bog, missed it, but sheared off the top of a scrub pine twenty feet beyond. Somehow (great reflexes?) he regained control and headed for Spruce Harbor International in his scarred but still functional aircraft.

As Lucinda told Hawkeye later, she and Trapper

were somewhat shaken by this experience. They lay, confused, scared and apart, looking up into the fog. "What happened?" Lucinda asked hesitantly, fearful of the answer.

"I'm not sure," replied Trapper. "Does the Church of the Nazarene have an air force?"

"I don't think so," mused Lucinda, regaining her composure. "That was Wrong Way Napolitano. I guess he must have seen us and had a muscle spasm, or something. Let's not worry."

"Speak to me of Wrong Way Napolitano," urged Trapper. "I know of him vaguely, but fill me in."

"Well, Hawkeye fixed a hernia for him a few months back and I got to know him. He's sort of a legend around here. He's really a very intelligent guy."

"That sounds like something Hawkeye told you."

"Well, yes. Hawk calls him a flaky dreamer, but everyone else laughs at him. They think of him as just a guy who runs a dinky little air service and spots schools of fish and flies people around the islands. Actually, Wrong Way could fly for any of the big airlines and, in fact, he does. Once or twice a month he disappears for a few days and fills in as pilot or copilot for Intercontinental. What's more, he could do that full time, but he likes it too well here."

"Do you mean this guy flies jets?"

Lucinda laughed. "Yes, he does. Hawkeye, like everybody, didn't really believe it until he went to Chicago for that course in vascular surgery a while back. You know how Hawkeye tells stories and blows them up a little, but I guess it was quite a shock to his nervous system."

"What happened?"

"If you want me to tell you, take your hand off my breast. It distracts me."

"Of course, my dear."

"Well, Hawkeye was a little late getting on this flight out of Logan to Chicago. Like every passenger, when he went aboard he peeked into the pilot's cabin. He was ten feet down the aisle before what he had seen registered. Sitting in the pilot's seat was Wrong Way Napolitano.

" 'Oh, no. It can't be,' Hawkeye said to the stewardess, and returned for a second look.

" 'It can't be what, sir?' asked the stewardess.

" 'Who's flying this thing?' Hawkeye asked.

" 'Captain Napolitano, sir.'

" 'Captain Napolitano, my ass,' said Hawkeye. 'Lemme off this mother.'

" 'I'm sorry, sir,' said the stewardess. 'It's too late.'

" 'You better believe it's too late,' Hawkeye said. 'Lemme talk to Wrong Way.'

" 'Who?'

" 'Captain Napolitano, if you insist.'

" 'I'm sorry, sir,' said the stewardess. 'You'll have to take your seat.'

" 'Okay," said Hawk, 'but honey, do both of us a favor, I beg you. Will you please go up forward, tell Captain Napolitano that Hawkeye Pierce is a passenger, and that I want to hear, directly from him, where we are going, and whether he's going to pay me for fixing his hernia or finish me off in a 707 to beat me out of my fee?'

"The stewardess followed instructions and came back with Wrong Way's Blue Shield card and a note which said: 'Chicago.' "

Seeing that Lucinda had finished her story. Trapper asked, "And that's who just ruined my morning love life?"

"Yes, indeed. Let us swim. Of course, Wooden Leg

expects us to peddle fish today. I hope Wrong Way got in okay. He hit that tree hard."

"But not square," Trapper pointed out. "Let's get going on Wooden Leg's fish."

Wrong Way Napolitano, with fear in his heart and trembling in his hands, landed his traumatized Tri-Pacer at Spruce Harbor International. Nothing gave way, a normal landing. Inspection of the plane revealed no major damage. Relieved, Wrong Way called the Massasoit Inn, a large summer hotel on Sears Point, a few miles east of Spruce Harbor. He asked to speak to the house dick, his best friend and brother-in-law, Tip Toe Tannenbaum. Whenever Wrong Way became overwrought he sought solace, advice and comfort from Tip Toe, a calm, judicious, meditative father of eight children, who was one of Spruce Harbor's most respected citizens.

Tip Toe, a tall, lean, black-haired, hawk-nosed soft-hearted middle-aged anachronism and deputy sheriff, had gradually achieved near saint status since his arrival in Spruce Harbor ten years earlier. Every summer he worked as security officer at the Massasoit for five hundred dollars a week, roughly five times the usual wage, because the management knew that Tip Toe was worth it one way or another. He solved all problems. He prevented theft. He protected the Inn from bad publicity. And parents of teen-age females knew that he never allowed teen-age females to get in trouble at the Massasoit Inn. Just having him around made everyone feel good.

During the nine months when the Massasoit Inn wasn't open, Tip Toe Tannenbaum disappeared every Sunday noon and reappeared the next Thursday noon. His wife Maria, sister of Wrong Way, always explained that he was away on business. "What business?" she was always asked. "He's a jet pilot," she would answer.

That was a perfect answer because, beyond the fact that Tip Toe was a great guy, the one thing everyone knew was that he was scared livid of airplanes. He would not go up in one. When his job as security officer at the Massasoit or deputy sheriff of Spruce County called for rapid reconnaissance of the area, Tip Toe chose boats or cars. This indeed occasionally became an embarrassment, but no one made an issue of it. One look at Tip Toe contemplating an airplane was enough.

Mrs. Tannenbaum drew smiles when she referred to "my husband the jet pilot." Lefty (a name he prefers to Luigi) Tannenbaum, the Androscoggin College quarterback and one of Tip Toe's sons, gracefully accepted everyone's disbelief when he alluded to "my father the jet pilot." Wooden Leg and Jocko, intimate friends of Tip Toe, always hailed Tip Toe in public as the left-handed Jewish jet pilot and explained to all who'd listen that left-handed Jewish jet pilots are scarce everywhere. The public, not fooled by all this foolishness, knew perfectly well that Tip Toe was the head of a large international detective agency.

Every Monday morning, except in summer, the pilot of Intercontinental Airways Flight 507 out of Idlewild to Paris and Rome was Captain Irving Tannenbaum, the house dick at the Massasoit Inn. The only people in Spruce Harbor who really knew this were Wrong Way Napolitano, his sister Mrs. Tannenbaum, the eight Tannenbaum children, Hawkeye, Wooden Leg, Jocko and Dr. Doggy Moore.

Tip Toe's career as a pilot hit bottom in 1954. The birth of his sixth child brought his fear of flying to a crescendo, so he went to Dr. Doggy Moore seeking help. If he'd gone to a psychiatrist he'd have been in trouble. Tip Toe wasn't foolish enough for that. A psychiatrist would have racked him up and advised him to find a different job. Not Doggy. "Look Tip Toe," he said, "you may be a little screwy here and there, but you're a valuable guy. If you're scared to fly, ain't nothin' I can do about it. Instead of bein' scared of flyin', why don't you concentrate on making your family rich?"

"Go on, Doggy," urged Tip Toe. "How do I do this?"

"They got them insurance machines in all the airports, don't they? Every time you go out, grab a million bucks of flight insurance."

There were initial difficulties because passengers, also seeking insurance, found their pilot camped at the insurance machines like a widow trying to beat a slot in Vegas. Later, a simple deduction from his paycheck provided Tip Toe with the million in insurance each time he went to Rome and back, and thereby avoided passenger discomfort. Tip Toe was able to fly happily with visions of his family rolling in wealth. He became one of Intercontinental's senior and most trusted pilots.

An hour after Wrong Way's abortive kamikaze attack on Thief Island an increasingly familiar, titillating spectacle was taking place on Spruce Harbor's main street. Wooden Leg's truck, filled with fish which had slept last night in Penobscot Bay, was parked in front of the Depositor's Trust Company. Trapper John—long-haired, bearded, in the briefest of swimming trunks—exuded charm and goodwill to all mankind as he deftly cut, to the customers' orders, fillets of haddock, cod and hake. The audience quivered as the suntanned, blonde Lucinda, draped in the scantiest of bikinis, packaged the ocean delights, made change and bequeathed a mind-blowing smile on each eager, happy customer.

On the edge of the crowd, as the truck emptied, stood Wooden Leg Wilcox and Tip Toe Tannenbaum.

"Business looks good," observed Tip Toe.

"Jesus, boy, betcher ever-lovin' A. The way them two move fish is some christly wondrous to behold."

"You hear what happened this morning?" asked Tip Toe.

"I heard Wrong Way hit a tree. So what else is new?"

"Reason he hit the tree was he saw Trapper and Lucinda working out in that cranberry patch. I guess he was distracted."

"Jesus Christ, Tip Toe," said Leg, "if that dumb guinea brother-in-law of yours has a few beers everybody in town will know about the cranberry patch."

"And," continued Tip Toe, "every darn plane for miles around will be circling Thief Island like gulls around a sardine boat. I think that would be too bad."

"So, what you gonna do? You gonna make Wrong Way keep quiet? That'll be the day."

"Well," mused Tip Toe, "I've had some thoughts. The new extension on the runway was finished last week. Wrong Way says they just got a supply of jet fuel. I think it's time for Spruce Harbor International to receive its first jet. Occasionally we need to refuel when Idlewild is stacked up or fogged in. What's more, the front office asked me to investigate the possibility of picking up two to three hundred pounds of fresh lobster meat if we came in here once a week. We like to feed our passengers the best. What are the possibilities, Leg?"

"Finestkind. I could give you a nice price and still

make a bundle. What's this got to do with Trapper and Lucinda?"

"Leg, the thought has come to my multidisciplined brain that Trapper and the young lady might prefer to perform exclusively for Intercontinental passengers, rather than be harassed by every private pilot on the coast of Maine. A suggestively erotic performance such as theirs would tend to alleviate our passengers' fear of an unscheduled landing at a small field."

"Suggestively erotic!" exclaimed Wooden Leg. "You mean if they'll take a piece when the jet comes in, you'll keep Wrong Way's mouth shut?"

"Precisely, Leg. One of our men is sick, so I have to go to Rome next week. Can you have the lobster meat ready about 5 P.M. next Thursday?"

"Betcher ass, Tip Toe. That'll shake 'em up. You bringing a 707 in here?"

"You don't know the half of it. Keep it under your hat, will you, Leg? I must talk to Lucinda."

"May I have a word with you two?" Tip Toe asked Trapper and Lucinda as the last fish was cut, packaged and paid for.

"Oh, hi," Lucinda said. "Trapper, this is Tip Toe Tannenbaum."

"A pleasure, Dr. McIntyre," said Tip Toe. "I'll just be a minute. I wanted to talk about this morning. Wrong Way told me all about it."

"Is this a pinch?" demanded Trapper.

"Good heavens, no, Doctor. Actually it's pure blackmail. I'm prepared to offer one hundred dollars per week for you two to perform exclusively for an Intercontinental Airways jet and if you don't agree, I'll let Wrong Way have four beers."

"What's that mean?" asked Trapper.

"After four beers," explained Lucinda, "Wrong Way keeps no secrets."

"I get it," said Trapper. "This way, we can hit the cranberries at will, just so we time one workout for Intercontinental. You mean you're going to bring a jet into that dinky airport? You mean, come to think of it, you're really a pilot?"

"Yes, sir," Tip Toe affirmed. "But not one word, understand?"

"Tip Toe," Lucinda said, "I'm ashamed of you." Then pausing, and with a coquettish grin, asked, "How high will you be over Thief?"

"Low enough for the passengers to get the idea. Too high for anyone to recognize you. I'm sure you will perform nobly. Your first assignment will be next Thursday at 4:50 P.M., weather permitting."

The Spruce Harbor fleet was annoyed on Monday when it learned that Wrong Way was not available for fish spotting. He left word that he would have to be away for several days but that he would be on duty Thursday evening. Schools of fish are most visible from the air in late evening when the wind has died down and dusk approaches. Wrong Way's occasional morning searches had borne no fish, only cranberries.

At 3:15 P.M. on Thursday consternation and havoc broke loose in the Spruce Harbor International control tower. Johnny Kimball, the flight controller, who had never seen a jet on the ground, received word from Air Traffic Control in Boston that Intercontinental flight 518 from Rome, Paris, now over Gander, would land at Spruce Harbor for refueling at approximately 1700 hours.

"Shit a jeezly goddamn," Johnny muttered, over and over. Everyone was hoping a jet would come, but no one really believed it would happen so soon or with so little warning.

Further information for Johnny was: "The aircraft will establish direct communication with you at approximately 1645 hours. Please be prepared with details of weather and landing instructions."

"I don't know what the hell to tell them," Johnny said, frantically and frankly.

"Have no fear," answered Air Traffic Control. "The pilot is familiar with your facilities."

Word spread from Johnny to a waitress in the cafeteria and to here and there. By 4:30 P.M. a crowd of hundreds had appeared to witness Spruce Harbor's first jet landing. Early arrivals were Maria Tannenbaum and her eight children who sat happily and proudly in, around and on top of the family station wagon. In the same area were Wooden Leg and Jocko Allcock. "Once the word is out, we're gonna clean up," Jocko kept saying. "Leg, you work the east side, I'll take the west."

At 4:45 P.M. communication was established between aircraft and control tower.

"Hello Spruce Harbor. How do things look? What's the wind doing?"

Johnny Kimball heard, and looked scared. "Ten to fifteen knots, 320 degrees," he said in scarcely more than a mumble.

"Okay," said the aircraft. "Is Cindy on duty?"

Cindy Howell was a tall redheaded University of Maine senior who'd been hostess and cashier in the cafeteria for the last month.

Johnny Kimball got pale before he turned green. "To whom am I talking?" he asked in a quavering voice.

"This is the copilot," answered the aircraft. "I know Spruce Harbor, so I'll be bringing this one in."

"What ails you, Johnny?" asked Cindy, who'd come up to bring him a cup of coffee.

"That voice," said Johnny, "that voice. It can't be, it just can't be."

More determined now, Johnny got back to the flight from Rome and demanded: "May I have the copilot's name, please?"

"This is the copilot, Captain Napolitano. Is there something wrong?"

Hawkeye Pierce, knowing it all in advance, had rushed through his office and arrived just in time to see Johnny Kimball running out of the control tower yelling: "Emergency. Get the fire trucks. Get ambulances. Get these people the hell out of here. Wrong Way's comin' in a 707."

The crowd now was restive but did not panic. Jocko and Wooden Leg circulated among the brave and curious, offering even money that Wrong Way would get in and out without mishap. Aware that Wrong Way had crash-landed something all over Spruce Harbor International, the crowd gave them plenty of action. Meanwhile Hawkeye walked into the deserted control tower where Captain Napolitano at five-second intervals was saying, "May I have landing instructions, please?"

Picking up the microphone, Hawkeye solemnly spoke to Captain Napolitano: "Here are your instructions. I repeat, here are your instructions. I will give them just once before I evacuate the area. Please repeat slowly after me: 'Our father, who art in heaven, hallowed be thy—' "

That was as far as he got before another voice interrupted: "Enough of that. Get off the radio, Hawkeye. Where's that idiot Kimball?"

"Right here," said Hawk, as Johnny, barely in control, returned to his post.

"Now listen very carefully, Kimball," said another voice. "This is Captain Tannenbaum. We will touch down at exactly 1700 hours. The passengers will disembark for one half hour. During that time I will take careful note of any remarks made, in the presence of my passengers, concerning the flying ability, personal habits, religion, other occupations or ethnic backgrounds of any member of my crew. Intercontinental giveth and Intercontinental can damn well taketh away. Is that clearly understood?"

"Huh!" replied Johnny.

"I'll explain it to him, Captain," said Hawkeye. "Just tell your copilot to keep his eyes on the runway and not on the cranberry bog."

"I'll try," said Tip Toe.

"Also," added Hawk, "there's a rifleman in the steeple of the Congo Church. The preach says they can't take a hit from a 707."

Aboard flight 518, five minutes before touchdown, a stewardess said over the intercom: "Ladies and gentlemen, shortly before landing at Spruce Harbor International, we will pass over Thief Island. This little island, now deserted, was for nearly two centuries the home of intrepid, hardy Maine fishermen. On the north edge of the island there is a tiny cranberry bog where, according to legend, local Indian tribes performed fertility rites before the coming of the white man. The idea in simple words seemed to be that consummation of the Indian brave's betrothal in this soft, warm bog assured him a long, happy, fruitful marriage. Intercontinental Airways is proud to present, for the exclusive enjoyment of its passengers, a reenactment of this ancient ritual. We regret that only the window seat passengers will have a clear view. Captain Tannenbaum suggests that a rearrangement of seating will allow for the others to view the ritual, which will be repeated upon our departure."

As the stewardess completed her commercial and thought that this sort of thing was out of character for Captain Tannenbaum, Hawkeye Pierce was talking to

Cindy, the long-legged redhead who was half-engaged to Wrong Way Napolitano.

"What's that song your boy's always playing on the jukebox?" he asked.

"Oh, you mean the 'Blue Water Line.' "

"Yeah. Play it as the plane comes in and hook it up to the loudspeaker. The Captain should be greeted by his theme song when he emerges triumphantly from the cockpit, or whatever you call it."

Flight 518, the passengers soothed by the reenactment of an ancient rite on Thief Island, set down smoothly at Spruce Harbor International Jetport and Captain Napolitano taxied to the terminal. The first thing the passengers heard as the door opened was Captain Napolitano's favorite line of his favorite song: "We'll have William Jennings Bryan stoking coal on number nine."

The local radio and TV people were there to interview the crew in the terminal lobby. The surprise of the communication industry's personnel was reflected in their performance. The first landing at Spruce Harbor was the news event of the decade. To discover that its pilots were local men added to its newsworthiness. To discover who they were was something else. The newsmen, of course, had covered previous exploits of Wrong Way and Tip Toe. To their credit they didn't blow it completely. The heroes, in the uniforms of Intercontinental, commanded automatic respect. Maria Tannenbaum, on TV, put her arm around Tip Toe and said: "Friends and neighbors, this is my husband the jet pilot." Cindy Howell, also on TV, embraced Captain Napolitano and answered a question which she'd been asked three times in the previous three weeks by announcing: "This is my fiancé the jet pilot."

Just before flight 518 took off for Idlewild, Wrong

Way's Uncle Pasquale, who'd stayed home with a hangover, approached his nephew and said: "Wrong Way, you sedda you was agonna spotta da fish tonight. You a very unreliable—"

"No, I'm not. Get on the radio. We got time to kill. Idlewild is stacked up. Tell the boys I'll give them fifteen minutes."

As 518 took off over Thief Island, Trapper John and Lucinda, stark naked, were running back and forth in the little field carrying a sheet which, in big red letters, cried: HELP!!

The stewardess then announced: "Ladies and gentlemen, we have just received word that our landing at Idlewild, due to circumstances beyond our control, will be delayed by twenty minutes. Captain Tannenbaum suggests that a look at the beautiful islands of Penobscot Bay from a height of twelve hundred feet rivals any scenery in the Bay of Naples. Accordingly we will spend a few minutes in this delightful area, rather than join the crowd and smog over New York."

Ten minutes later, although Wrong Way had spotted three large schools of herring, the word came from below: "Hey, a Wrong Way. You getta that bigga noisamaka the hell outa here. You gonna scara da fish."

Later, when the weekly Intercontinental jet flight to Spruce Harbor became a regular thing, Wooden Leg Wilcox, enjoying a beer at the Bay View Café with the two flyers, said: "I gotta admit, for a guinea kamikaze pilot and a left-handed Hebe, you guys have done okay."

10

Late in the afternoon of August 14, 1959, Hawkeye and Mary Pierce, on their way to the Gaspé Peninsula, checked into the Golden View Motel in Dalhousie, New Brunswick, after six hours of hot-weather driving. They quickly put on swimsuits and ran for the beach in front of the motel. Comforted, a few minutes later, by the cool water of the Bay of Chaleur, they lay on a beach blanket and sipped cold beer.

"Don't forget," said Mary, "you promised if you ever got to Dalhousie, you'd call on Laurie."

"I say lots of things. What the hell. That was two years ago."

"You are going to call on Laurie Kirkaldy and that's all there is to it."

"Yeah, but Jesus."

"Now look, Hawkeye," Mary said, "you know how he'd feel if he ever found out you were here and hadn't called."

"Yeah. I'd like to see him, but maybe he won't want to see me."

"Don't be foolish."

Mary and Hawkeye had dinner in the motel dining room. A calendar on the wall of the tiny bar which guarded the entrance to the dining room offered the drinking public a nearly nude damsel, with the best regards of Kirkaldy's Insurance Agency, Dalhousie, N. B.

"Helluva picture," said Hawkeye to the bartender as they entered. "Is that why they call New Brunswick the Picture Province?"

"Sir?" inquired the bartender.

"Two Beefeater Marts on the rocks," replied Hawkeye.

"Yes, sir."

When the bartender brought the martinis Hawkeye asked: "Do you know the Mr. Kirkaldy who provided you with that fine picture?"

"Aye, sir. Everyone knows Laurie."

"How's he hittin' em?"

"Sir?"

"How's his golf game?"

"Oh, topnotch, sir. Not like in the old days afore the sickness, but not many can beat him."

"Do you play?" Hawkeye asked the bartender.

"Aye, sir."

"What's your handicap?"

"Ten, sir."

"How do you play Laurie? You get strokes from him?"

"Aye. Three to a side. Six in eighteen holes."

"That's what I'm going to get. Where's he live?"

"Two twenty Chatham Street."

While they ate, Mary was silent for a while and then prodded Hawkeye: "Tell me again about Laurie and golf."

"Well," he said, "Laurie was born about 1914 in a place called Denhead, near Saint Andrews, Scotland. By the time he was ten he was caddying on the Old Course, and he is related to Andrew Kirkaldy, who was once the Honorary Professional at the Royal and Ancient Golf Club. He emigrated to Canada when he was twenty-two and tried to make a living out of golf. He became a greenskeeper first, then a pro, but found that golf in Canada is not like golf in Scotland, where you can play the year around. So he learned the insurance business and became successful. He played enough golf to remain the best golfer in Dalhousie, and he sells a lot of insurance on the golf course."

After dinner Hawkeye and Mary drove, slowly, along Chatham Street, looking for 220, which was a small, well-kept house with a neat front lawn and a cookout rig in the backyard. All the houses on Chatham Street seemed similarly equipped. Hawkeye drove his dirty, bent-fendered station wagon into Laurie's driveway. A bit nervously, he went to the front door and knocked.

It was quite clear that no one was home, but Hawk went through the motions. He had noticed a lady in the next yard weeding her garden. Aware that she was watching him, he walked toward her and asked: "Does Laurie Kirkaldy live here?"

"You're the doctor who operated on Laurie, aren't you?" she asked.

In the background Mary Pierce heard the neighbor's question and emitted a sort of whoop.

Hawkeye Pierce's immediate unvoiced answer was, "Lady, you some kind of a christly nut? I'm just a guy in old clothes and I need a haircut. I drove into Laurie's yard in a beat-up station wagon and you ain't even seen the license plates so what the hell makes me the guy who operated on Laurie?"

What he actually said was, "Yes, I'm Laurie's doctor."

"I knew it!" she said. "I'm Mrs. MacTavish. We've been neighbors to Laurie and Bertha for twenty years."

"Do you think every stranger is the man who operated on Laurie?"

"No indeed, Doctor, but Laurie told me you'd be by one day and that you were tall and nice-looking and wouldn't be acting like a doctor. So, I just knew. Laurie's at his cottage at the beach. I'll send my daughter," offered Mrs. MacTavish, "but she won't be home for half an hour."

"Tell Laurie we're at the Golden View and we'll be expecting him and Bertha."

"Oh, he'll be so happy," exclaimed Mrs. MacTavish.

As the Pierces rode slowly back to the Golden View Motel, Mary saw tears in the corners of her husband's eyes.

"Why does this guy get to you?" she asked. "Every time you think of Laurie Kirkaldy you start crying."

"His was a special kind of case and he's a special kind of guy. In a sense, Laurie did more for me than I did for him. He had such complete faith that I'd get him well that he sort of inspired me to get him well. The fact that he didn't die made me a confident surgeon and, to be commercial, a lot of the material success we're enjoying now has come to us just because Laurie and I got lucky together."

"I'm not sure you make sense all the time, Hawkeye. You saved Laurie after Ramsey Coffin almost killed him and then you used that as an excuse to destroy Ramsey Coffin. At least, that's a common version of the story."

"So you're still not sure whether I'm the hero or the villain?"

"Frankly, no. A lot of people still blame you for Ramsey Coffin's having to leave town. Maybe you should tell me about it."

"In addition to his other shortcomings, Ramsey

Coffin had square toes, like he never had a bad lie in the rough."

"Do you hate everyone who cheats at golf?" asked Mary.

"If you don't shut up, I'll rape you in the motel swimming pool."

"Never mind that," said Mary. "Give me your latest version of the story before we meet Laurie and Bertha."

"Well," said Hawkeye, driving even more slowly, "Laurie and Bertha were visiting Bertha's niece and her family in Eagle Head in August, 1957. There was a clambake. Laurie, his golf game in trim, his insurance business growing, his waistline burgeoning, was playing the role of perfect guest. He partook of clams, lobsters, corn, beer and Scotch whiskey. What was it? The last lobster claw? The last ear of corn? Who knows? Suddenly Laurie had too much of something and felt sick. Before he could retreat to privacy he vomited, violently, in his niece's back yard. 'My God,' he yelled, and fell to the ground, clawing at his chest. Searing breathtaking pain radiated upward into his neck and jaw, into his shoulders, down his arms. Laurie writhed on the ground and begged for help.

"Laurie's niece, Nancy Barnes, knew that it's quicker to drive four miles in the area of Eagle Head than to make a phone call so she jumped into her car, drove to the home of Tony Holcombe, found him mowing his lawn and gave him the word. Tony responded by mounting his station wagon and driving to Nancy's house with the enthusiasm, if not the skill, of Stirling Moss. Tony decided correctly that Laurie had ruptured his esophagus, the tube that leads to the stomach. Tony prepared a syringeful of Demerol to give intravenously. He told Nancy to call the hospital, that immediate surgery was necessary and to get hold of Dr. Pierce. That's me."

"I know," Mary agreed.

"Tony Holcombe arrived with Laurie on a mattress in the back of his black-and-yellow station wagon. 'Let's get him directly to the OR,' Tony said to the supervisor, Minnie Morse, and asked, 'Have you located Dr. Pierce?'

" 'Dr. Pierce is on the golf course, but Dr. Coffin is here,' Minnie told him.

" 'My good woman,' said Tony, 'I know you haven't called the golf course because I imagine you wouldn't roll over in bed without a list of instructions. Right now, send someone to the golf course and get Dr. Pierce.'

"At this point, just when the need was for action, not talk, Goofus MacDuff, the Mighty Medical Director, intruded. He'd come in on Sunday afternoon to pursue his hobby of finding out which doctors were delinquent in their records. His contribution to this act was to say, 'I don't see why you need Pierce. Dr. Coffin is on surgical call. Why not let him handle it?'

" 'Because,' replied Tony, 'Dr. Coffin is not a thoracic surgeon and Dr. Pierce is and this is a total, classic thoracic surgical emergency and the patient's life depends on everything being done properly. Even you should understand this.'

" 'You can't talk to me that way,' said Goofus.

"I think Tony might have stolen two minutes to clean Goofus's clock at this point had not Jocko Allcock and Half A Man Timberlake arrived. Jocko had seen Tony's wagon going fast and followed. As usual he took command. To Half A Man he said: 'Hawkeye's probably on the sixteenth. Wherever he is find him and get his ass in here or it's going to be your ass. Take my car and hurry."

"Well, hell, you know Half A Man. Six feet and two inches of gorgeous thirty-five-year-old male with an I.Q. of eighty and a total preoccupation with sex. He's Jocko's main man and Jocko gets him laid often enough to blunt his horns and usually Half A Man performs routine chores with more enthusiasm and efficiency than normal people. But the ride to the country club took Half A Man past that whorehouse on Elm Street. Bette Bang-Bang, Mattress Mary and Made Marion were sitting on the front porch sipping gin and tonic because Sunday afternoons are slow for them. They spotted Half A Man and yelled. Half A Man heard and all else left the small compartment of his brain which could be described as his mind. The girls did him up brown while I had two drinks in the clubhouse and went on home, with no inkling that I was the most wanted man in the area."

Hawkeye told Mary this much of the story on the way back to the Golden View, where they mixed some rum and bitter orange, sat on the back porch of their motel room and watched the moon shine on the tranquil Bay of Chaleur.

"This was ridiculous, of course," said Mary, as the story continued. "They could have found you. They could have called everywhere, alerted the police. It wasn't as though you'd been swallowed up."

"Yes, but remember the confusion. Tony and Me Lay thought I'd be right there so they put Laurie to sleep. Meanwhile Old Wiley Morgan, the fearless one, had arrived. When I didn't show, they let Coffin and Morgan have a go at it. They made a hole in Laurie's chest about four inches too high, got out a few kernels of corn and a little Scotch whisky. Laurie got better, so they figured they were heroes."

"And then?" asked Mary.

"Then it started to get complicated. Tony told Mrs.

Kirkaldy's niece, Nancy Barnes, that I should take over, but Nancy, like so many broads, was under Ramsey's spell. Tony was a foreigner, I was a newcomer, and Goofus told her Laurie was Dr. Coffin's case and that I wasn't needed."

"But you did get to Laurie, didn't you?"

"Yes. Three days later he had a temperature of 105, a pulse of 150, a falling blood pressure and everyone but Ramsey was taking the choke. Ramsey was calmly telling the family that Laurie couldn't possibly make it and that any further surgery would kill him. Tony, meanwhile, was telling the family that if I wasn't called in he'd never attend any of them again. So I decided to take over, regardless of who liked it."

"Shouldn't you have done that earlier?" asked Mary.

"Sure, but I'd been in practice just a year or so. I'd know what to do now, but back then I was just spinning my wheels when I should have been moving."

"As I recall," said Mary, "when you decided to move you did it in your usual crude way."

"I guess. Obviously the guy couldn't live unless something was done, so when Tony gave me the word I scheduled Laurie for surgery and didn't bother to talk to anyone. I knew I might kill him and if I did there'd be hell to pay. Goofus and Ramsey swooped down on me and I told Goofus that if he made one sound I'd deck him and I told Ramsey that he was a mealymouthed phony and that I was going to get him sooner or later."

"How was that received?"

"I was too concerned with the main issue to assess peasant reaction. Would you like to hear about the operation?"

"Yes."

"Well, Me Lay put Laurie to sleep and said, 'Whatever you're going to do, do it quick.' As I told you, Ramsey had made the incision much too high. I ripped out his tenth rib and scooped out lobsters, clams and corn. There was a big hole in the lower esophagus. I sewed this up even though I knew it wouldn't stay closed because you simply can't get healing at this stage of the game. I established good dependent drainage and then we flipped him onto his back and made a hole in his belly and stuck a tube in the beginning of the small bowel so we could feed him. I didn't spend over forty minutes doing all this and Laurie was better even before the operation was over. He had the wherewithal to survive. There was a long haul ahead but we started a winning game that morning."

"Postoperatively," asked Mary, "did you take a moment to assess peasant reaction?"

"Not really. When Laurie came out of the OR alive, Ramsey and Goofus were some upset, but I ignored both of them except to give Ramsey a look which indicated that I intended to bear him in mind."

"That was when you decided to destroy him, wasn't it?" insisted Mary.

"I wish for Chrissake you'd stop using that word *destroy*. I just decided to study him in depth and find a way to separate him from the local surgical scene. This was a completely justified and reasonable decision. I know that everyone blames me for it because so many of your dumb friends thought he was a christly saint."

"What, exactly, did you do?"

"First, I made sure that what Me Lay had told me about his training was true. He'd have needed two more years of formal training just to qualify for the American Board of Surgery. Still, at Workmen's Compensation hearings he described himself as Board-certified."

"So," said Mary, "he lied about his training?"

"Yes. Then I went over everything he'd done since he'd been in practice. He made out like a tall dog jerking normal gallbladders and uteri. I satisfied myself that he was totally incompetent."

"Even by Spruce Harbor standards at the time?"

"Yes. Old Wiley Morgan was better, but Ramsey had the come on."

"I still don't see where this got you," said Mary. "The hospital didn't require specialized training then and he wasn't the only one around doing unnecessary hysterectomies. You must have found something else."

"I did, indeed," said Hawkeye with a pleased smirk. "Ramsey seemed to be large with the broads. He had that Jaguar and a speedboat and an airplane. He was single, young, good-looking and he should have been getting enough to kill three men. I learned that Ramsey could hack it only with married women."

"And how did you find that out?"

"I heard it from Bette Bang-Bang."

"You *do* swing in High Society, don't you?" said Mary.

"Bette Bang-Bang is a very basic person. She told me that Ramsey flunked out with her and Mattress Mary and Made Marion. But stick him in bed with a married amateur and he was a tiger. You never tried him, did you?"

"Oh go to hell. Before you tell me more of that sordid story. I want to hear about Laurie and what happened to him."

"Well, once I had his chest drained properly, he stabilized. We fed him through the tube in his bowel and he didn't need intravenous fluids, but four days after surgery it became clear that the hole in his esophagus had reopened, as I'd known it would."

"What did you do?"

"Nothing to do. I gave nature time. I figured if he could heal it himself it'd be better than a surgical attempt. This meant nothing by mouth. Not even swallow his spit. Anything that went by that hole in his esophagus delayed healing so I came on strong with him. Laurie kept saying, 'So help me God, Hawkeye, if I ever get well enough to go home to New Brunswick, I'm going to stop at every stream along the way and have a drink of cool, clear water."

"I kept telling him how I hate golf pros and that I was going to make him suffer. The banter made it easier for both of us, but Laurie suffered and you better believe it. I made up my mind to play it cool and conservative—even when X-rays seemed to show that the hole had closed. I kept him on nothing by mouth for six weeks."

"That's awful," Mary proclaimed.

"I know. Finally, two months after he'd ruptured his esophagus I closed the jejunostomy—where we'd fed him—and sent him home. His chest X-ray still looked lousy, but he was feeling better and gaining weight. He got along well until about February—six months after it all started—and then he developed empyema in his left chest."

"What's that?"

"Pus, baby. It was an unholy mess and it meant three more months in the hospital and three more operations, the last of which was taking out his left lower lobe. He's had minor trouble since, but he's okay. Maybe his golf game has suffered a little. I don't know about that."

"Get back to Ramsey," ordered Mrs. Pierce, after Hawkeye had mixed two new drinks.

"Well, I remembered what Bette Bang-Bang told me about Ramsey and married women, so I called her in consultation. She was reluctant to cooperate but there are certain legal irregularities in her business, which I pointed out, so she came through. She didn't know just which marriages Ramsey was tapping into, but she knew her customers, one of whom was Joe Harkness, that shylock from the Mutual Trust who's on the board of directors of the hospital."

"Oh," said Mary. "I knew his wife Beth in college. A nice girl."

"Ramsey Coffin agreed with you. I arranged for the next dose of clap in Bette's organization to go untreated until it had been handed onto Joe Harkness. Before he knew he had it, he'd given it to Beth who anointed Ramsey who then passed the baton to Ruth Cox and so on. Pretty soon we had the greatest venereal ring-around-the-rosy you've ever seen."

"God, you're awful," commented Mrs. Pierce.

"I know," Hawkeye agreed happily. "Pretty soon Doggy Moore was treating half a dozen nonclap type females for clap, and he was getting awful curious. Duke and I were treating the husbands, most of whom had guilty consciences. If they didn't, we told them that they had a nonvenereal infection. So only the wives had to go for help to Doggy.

"You know that Doggy's a real bulldog. The second time Ruth Cox came in with a dose he pinned her right to the wall and refused to treat her until she told him where she got it. Ruth was scared and told him. For the next two or three months Doggy asked every nonclap female if she'd been to bed with Ramsey Coffin and they all admitted it."

"What did he do?"

"When he put it all together he blew the whistle, and that was the end of Ramsey Coffin in Spruce

Harbor. Eight outraged husbands gave Ramsey the word."

"You actually enjoyed yourself. That bothers me," said Mary.

"I gotta admit I did. We couldn't keep score with perfect accuracy, but the way we had it going we could figure pretty closely when Ramsey would diagnose his own illness. Every time he got a new dose Duke had Little Eva tail him for a couple of days. I think this tore it for Ramsey. That bloodhound was getting to him. Duke has claimed ever since that Little Eva is the only dog in the world that can diagnose the clap. Ramsey left town, I'm sure, hating all bloodhounds."

"Truly a moving tale," Mary said. "There's someone at the door. I think Laurie and Bertha are here."

The meeting of the Pierces and the Kirkaldys was a touch strained at first, but Mary and Bertha had common interests in teaching and Hawkeye and Laurie had a common interest in Scotch whisky and lauding each other's virtues. So the evening ended sentimentally and convivially with a golf game planned for the morning. It was 11:30 P.M. when the door of the motel room opened, shedding light on a Pontiac from Saskatchewan. Out came Laurie Kirkaldy and Hawkeye followed by their wives. Laurie and Hawkeye were half in the bag and hugging each other and weeping a little as half-in-baggers are inclined to do.

"You'd better drive, Bertha," Hawkeye advised Mrs. Kirkaldy, the still pretty middle-aged schoolteacher he'd spent so much time consoling two years earlier, "and don't let him stop at any streams. He'd likely drown."

At the Dalhousie Country Club at 9 A.M. the next morning, there was a degree of dishonesty. Hawkeye, who'd whittled his handicap down to five in 1958, had played little and poorly in 1959, and had a card from Wawenock Harbor attesting to a ten handicap. For a week prior to this Canadian trip, however, he had practiced as though he had been invited to the Crosby, and was hitting the ball very well. Laurie Kirkaldy, on the first tee, lamented that ever since his extensive surgery with multiple incisions and loss of half a lung, his swing had been impaired and that he, himself, suffered the indignity of a five handicap.

"Look, you Scotch thief," said Hawkeye. "I got you right where I want you. The bartender at the Golden View is a ten and you give him six blows. That's what I want and that's what I'm going to get."

"Och, mon!" protested Laurie. "The bartender is Bertha's cousin and it's in the family and he has five kids. It's an act of charity."

"Six blows, Laurie, or I continue my trip to the Gaspé Peninsula right here and now."

"I suppose I owe you for saving my life," said Laurie unhappily. "Six it is."

Hawkeye Pierce, not really a good golfer, particularly on a strange course, had one of his best days. He shot seventy-six. Laurie Kirkaldy shot sixty-seven and won fifteen dollars from Hawkeye.

While Laurie, Mary and Bertha found a table in the dining room, Hawkeye went to the pro shop, realizing that he should have done this before, not after the match.

"What's Kirkaldy's handicap?" he asked the pro.

"Laurie? Oh, sir, he plays at scratch and he's often under par. I hope you get strokes from him, sir."

"I got six strokes, shot seventy-six, and lost," said Hawkeye.

"What a shame," observed the pro.

Returning to lunch, Hawkeye told Mary: "Lunch

and drinks are on this Scotch thief. Order the most expensive thing on the menu."

Laurie Kirkaldy chuckled. "Eat, Hawkeye, and enjoy it," he said. "You'll never know what a delight it is until you've been denied the privilege."

11

Tedium Cove Wharf was quiet. Seagulls cried in the background. A lobster boat idled, unloading the morning catch.

July fifth was a sunny morning with little wind. A lobsterman leaned against the wharf railing, smoking, looking across the harbor. He appeared to be lost in deep thought. Actually, he was just lost.

A large young man, in his late twenties or early thirties, wearing Bermuda shorts, walked with the bouncy stride of either a birdwatcher or an associate professor of sociology. He approached the lobsterman and said: "Good morning, sir. Isn't this a fine morning?"

"Ayuh. Finestkind."

"Are you a lobsterman?"

"Ayuh."

"How's the fishing these days?"

"Wouldn't dast say."

"But aren't you a fisherman?"

"Give it up. Just go lobsterin'."

"I see. My name is Jim Russell. I'm in the sociology

department at the University of Maine. I'm making a study of people in the lobster and fishing industry."

"You be?"

"Ahuh—I mean, yes, sir, I am."

"You know Zeke Simmons's boy?"

"No, I'm afraid I don't. Does he go to the University?"

"Claims to."

"What's he studying?"

"He ain't."

"I don't understand."

"I don't neither. He ain't learnt nawthin' 'cept how to jerk bulls."

"I'm afraid I still don't understand."

"Gawd, boy, I don't neither. He be interferin' with nature."

"Oh, now I get it. He must be in the agricultural course, learning about artificial insemination."

"Ayuh. By Gawd, Zeke says they don't none of them Spanish bullfighters hold a candle to this boy. 'Tain't nawthin' to wave a blanket at some bull and stab him with one of them swords compared to ———"

"Really, sir, I don't believe this is done in quite the way you imagine."

"It ain't? Gawd, boy, I dunno. Zeke says some bull knocked his boy toes up. He failed the test."

"I'm afraid I don't know what you mean by toes up."

"Jeezly bull knocked him ahss over teakettle. They hauled him off toes up. By Gawd, I guess that bull musta thought Zeke's boy was some queeah. Wish't I coulda seen it."

"I'm sure it would have been very interesting. By the way, sir, may I ask your name?"

"Ben Simmons."

"Well, it's a pleasure to know you, Mr. Simmons."

"I shouldn't wondah."

"I would be pleased if you'd be willing to tell me a little about yourself, your life here in Tedium Cove, your family and so forth."

"You figure to settle heah, boy?"

"No, sir, I'd just like to ask some questions. Do you mind?"

"Dunno till I hear the questions."

"Could we sit down somewhere and be comfortable?"

"You got any beah?"

"No, but I'll get some, if you'll tell me where I can buy it."

"You can git some off'n George."

"Where can I find George?"

"To the stowah, right over theah. Better git a six-pack."

"Yes, sir. I'll be right back."

Ten minutes later James Russell, Associate Professor of Sociology, returned to find Ben Simmons just where he had left him.

"Well, now, Mr. Simmons, here's a nice cool one. Open it up and let's get down to business. Do you mind if I take a few notes?"

"Gawd, ain't that some good! You got another one handy?"

"Oh, certainly, Mr. Simmons. My, but you drank that quickly."

"Gawd, boy, I don't drink the fust one. I just kinda pour her into me."

"How old are you, Mr. Simmons?"

"I wouldn't dast say."

"You mean you don't even know your age? How can this be?"

"I dunno."

"Well, don't you know your birthday?"

" 'Course I do. April 21."

"Well, in what year were you born?"

"Dunno. Never give it no thought. It was backalong."

"Well, don't you have any idea? I'd say you might be about forty-five years old."

"I shouldn't wondah."

"Tell me about your family, Mr. Simmons. Do you have children?"

"Ahuh."

"How many?"

"Wouldn't dast say."

"Mr. Simmons, I've interviewed a lot of people. I don't believe I've ever found anyone quite as secretive as you. You seem to evade a direct answer even to the simplest questions. I'll bet you wouldn't even give me the right time.

"I said I bet you wouldn't even give me the right time."

"How in hell you know? You ain't asked."

"Okay, I'll ask. What time is it?"

"Dunno."

"Why not, Mr. Simmons? I see a watch on your wrist."

" 'Tain't set right. She gains and I ain't set her for goin' on a week. She gains maybe a minute most every day."

"What's your watch say now?"

" 'Bout twenty-two minute past ten."

"Then it's safe to say that the time is approximately ten fifteen."

"Shouldn't wondah. Wouldn't dast say fuh showah. Why? Be you in a hurry to git somewheah?"

"No, certainly not, Mr. Simmons. Let's get back to

your children. How can you say you don't know how many you have?"

"Gawd, boy, you can't believe nawthin' around heah. How in hell would I know how many I got? I got ten to home, then there's three away and there's some I got credit for but a feller can't tell 'bout them things."

"What do you mean by 'away,' Mr. Simmons? Do you have three children who've moved away from Tedium Cove?"

"Gawd, no. They live in the Cove, right to home. One of them belongs to a widder woman who was sufferin' some awful and Jess Simmons's two kids is mine. Jess ain't no good, so I helped him out."

"How's Jess feel about this?"

"Dunno. I ain't never asked him."

"Does he know that you are the father of his children?"

"Gawd, ain't you some curious?"

"I beg your pardon, Mr. Simmons. Can you tell me about your wife?"

"Ahuh. Which one?"

"You mean you have more than one?"

"Gawd, boy, you take me for a jeezly Mormon? Cuss I ain't. My fust one left me."

"Oh, I'm sorry. Do you mind talking about it?"

"Damn fool woman fell overboard off'n Wreck Island whilst we was a haulin' traps. 'Twas one of them foggy days. I never see hide nor hair of her agin."

"Did she drown?"

"More'n likely."

"Well, didn't you recover the body?"

"Coast Guard found her in sixteen foot of water off'n Dutch Neck. They was ten lobsters muckled onto her. They called and asked my instructions. 'Git them lobsters off'n her and set her agin,' I says."

Ben liked to embellish this story and see how the summer complaints reacted but Mr. Russell, overcome by the enormity of it, or something, simply said, "I'm very sorry, Mr. Simmons. When did you remarry?"

"Oh, not for a while. I musta held off three or four month."

"I see. How many children did you have by your first wife?"

"I should imagine five or six."

"Really, Mr. Simmons. Oh, well, never mind. So you've had, then, four or five by your second wife?"

"Gawd, no. She only had two after we was married, but she claims the ones she come with was mine."

"Mr. Simmons, I get the idea that marriage is a rather flexible arrangement in this community."

"Gawd, boy, a feller got to have a little on the side. How 'bout another one of them beuh?"

"Oh, of course. Tell me, Mr. Simmons, how many lobster traps do you have?"

"I wouldn't dast say."

"Oh, for Chrissake. I mean, can you give me some idea?"

"I got either one hundred and ninety or one hundred ninety-one, that I can find."

A colleague, John Simmons, entered the scene. "Hi, Ben. How be yuh?"

"Finestkind."

"Hey, Ben, I hear you been gittin' something more'n food off'n that new cook over to the Inn."

"Feller can hear most anythin' if'n he listens."

"I hear she's a mite smooth on the tooth but right stemmy."

"I wouldn't dast say, John."

"Do any good this mornin', Ben?"

"Got enough to pay my gas. Didn't need no moah. Feller from the college to Orono bought me a six-pack.

That'll get me through the mornin'. John, this here's Mr. Russell."

"How do you do, John. I assume your last name is Simmons."

"Gawd, you college fellers is some smart. How'd you ever know that?"

"It was an educated guess."

"Well, I be goddamned. You stayin' to the Inn, Mr. Russell?"

"Ayuh—I mean, yes, I am. A very nice place. The rooms are pleasant and the food is delicious."

"Ayuh. They got a finestkind cook, or so I heah. You seen her?"

"Yes, I have. I've had several pleasant conversations with her."

"Gawd, boy, if'n you get a chance, I wish't you'd put in a good word for me. You kin tell her Ben Simmons don't hold no candle to the likes of John Simmons."

"John, 'tain't candles she likes," offered Ben Simmons.

"Well, gentlemen, I really don't think our cook would care to have me intercede, one way or another, in her off-duty time. I'm sure that between the two of you she'll be well taken care of."

"Ayuh!" (Ben Simmons)

"Ayuh." (John Simmons)

"So long, Ben. So long. Mr. Russell. I gotta take my woman to the hospital. She's due to calve most anytime now."

"Well, Ben, perhaps we could get on with our discussion."

"If'n you've a mind to. I better have another one of them beah afore she cools off."

"Of course, Ben. Can you tell me something about the religious life of your community?"

"Professor, you come direct to the right feller."

"You mean you can tell me about the Tedium Cove Church? Frankly, I'm surprised."

"Well now, don't misunderstand me, boy. I'm a lot better acquainted to the parsonage than I be to the church. They only got church one day a week, but the Reverend's got a young missus who spreads the gospel seven day a week while the Reverend, he goes to visit sick folks and others. By Gawd, religion has come on strong since them two come."

"I'm afraid I don't understand."

"The Reverend Titcomb and his missus is both of them hornier than a three-ball tomcat. Religion done took right aholt in Tedium Cove."

"What denomination are they?"

"They's Rollers. By Gawd, they beat hell out of them Baptists we had afore. Swimmin' ain't never goin' to catch on around heah."

"I see, I think. You mean the minister's wife actually—"

"Oh, Gawd, boy, finestkind."

"That's very interesting."

"It's some good, too."

A small cabin cruiser pushed by a big Mercury outboard approached the wharf. Hawkeye Pierce jumped from the bow, rope in hand, tied up, and hoped to negotiate with the natives for gasoline.

"Be that you, Hawkeye?" yelled Ben Simmons, who'd needed his appendix out during the winter.

"Ben! How be yuh?" asked Hawkeye. "You getting much?"

"*You* might call it a lot," Ben answered modestly.

"I'm sure I would."

"Hey, Hawkeye, I wantcha to meet Mr. Russell. He's from the college to Orono."

"I'm Dr. Hawkeye Pierce, Mr. Russell," explained

Hawkeye. "I had the pleasure of removing Ben's appendix awhile back. Unfortunately the ethics of my profession forced me to stop there."

"I think I know what you mean," said Mr. Russell.

"Ayuh," said Ben Simmons. "By Jesus, I think I may go up to the parsonage."

"I hear there's action there," said Hawkeye. "Is it true the Reverend is a marriage counselor, in addition to his other activities?"

"You might say," agreed Ben, "But I ain't heard of him counselin' no couples. Mostly he just counsels the female and you gotta figure he ain't too bad. Lotta young folks been stayin' together, just so long as the Reverend can keep on makin' mornin' calls. Hung, he is."

"I'm sure," agreed Hawkeye. "The faith is kept in many ways."

Ben Simmons, a six-pack in him, aimed for the parsonage, leaving Mr. Russell and Hawkeye Pierce in the bright sunshine on Tedium Cove Wharf.

"I just don't know what to make of that man," exclaimed Mr. Russell.

"That's just because you weren't born and brought up around here," said Hawkeye. "He may not be the exact average, but he's not unusual either."

"He's an animal," exclaimed Mr. Russell.

"Perhaps more overtly than you and me, Mr. Russell, but quantitatively not much more. If I knew where I could get a good piece of tail half an hour from now, with no trouble from it, I'd get it. Probably you would, too."

"But a minister's wife!" persisted Mr. Russell.

"Think a little, Mr. Russell. A minister in Tedium Cove, whatever his denominational handle, has to be very dumb or very something else with rare exceptions. I happen to know that the Reverend and Mrs. Titcomb are treated for venereal disease about once a month. I'd say that they are dumb and something else, too. I'll leave the final evaluation of this to you, since you're a sociologist."

"I must admit I'm out of my element," said Professor Russell. "I can't really believe this sort of thing goes on. Well, I mean, I know it goes on, but is Ben Simmons going to just walk up to the parsonage and go to bed with the minister's wife?"

"Depends on the length of the line," said Hawkeye.

"Hi, Hawkeye," came the voice of John Simmons. "By Jesus, Hawk, I was gonna take my woman to the hospital soon as I got through haulin' but she come on quick and the State Police took her in. I got me a new daughter."

"Congratulations, John. How do you plan to celebrate?

"I been broken off, except to the parsonage, for three month. Maybe I'll up and go git me a hunk of religion."

"Good luck, John," offered Hawkeye.

"Good Lord," exclaimed Mr. Russell. "Ben Simmons and John Simmons are both heading for the parsonage."

"Could be sociologically significant. Why don't we see what happens?" Dr. Pierce suggested.

"Oh, my," said Mr. Russell.

As they approached the parsonage they heard three voices, all loud, all outraged. "What on earth is happening?" gasped Professor Russell, breaking into a gallop.

"Hold her up, Professor. Sounds like Mrs. Titcomb is defending her virtue."

They approached warily, mounted the front porch

and peeked through a window into the spacious living room of the old parsonage where Ben and John Simmons were thrashing about, threatening each other with death and mutilation. Mrs. Titcomb, armed with a baseball bat, circled warily and bided her time. Swish went the bat, not too hard but not too soft, on John Simmons's head, and the lights went out for the proud parent.

"By Gawd, Jenny, you got him good, you did," applauded Ben Simmons. "Let's get busy afore he comes to."

There was a dull thud as Jenny Titcomb, apparently disenchanted with Ben Simmons, carefully brought the baseball bat to bear on his right temporal area. Ben joined John in dreamland.

"Oh, my God, my God," wailed Professor Russell.

"This is real basic sociology, Professor," said Hawkeye. "I hope you're taking notes. That broad has a sweet swing. Reminds me of Musial, the way she holds it up high waiting for a shot."

"What'll we do?"

"I suppose we have to take these base hits to the hospital."

Opening the screen door leading to the batting cage, Hawkeye walked in, followed by a trembling professor of sociology, and said: "Congratulations, Mrs. Titcomb. You are two for two. I'm Dr. Pierce. Professor Russell and I happened to be passing and heard the commotion. I guess maybe I'd better take over. These gentlemen could be seriously injured, although it's unlikely since you hit them both in the head."

"Oh, the Lord help me," requested Jenny Titcomb.

"I don't know about Him, but I will, Jenny. Under the circumstances it'll be easy for me and the Professor to testify that Ben and John knocked each other out, if anyone cares enough to ask, which isn't likely.

"What do you have for wheels, Professor?" asked Hawkeye, as he examined the victims and decided that although unconscious and in need of care, they'd probably recover.

"A station wagon," said the Professor.

"Get it, and we'll take these fallen athletes to the hospital."

As Professor Russell drove Hawkeye and the fallen athletes to Spruce Harbor General, Hawkeye was bemoaning his fate. "Wouldn't you know it?" he complained. "I take a day off, just put in for some gas and the first thing you know I'm working again."

"You seem more concerned about your day off than the lives of two men," said Professor Russell.

"That's where you peripheral thinkers always blow it, Professor. Once in the hospital, they'll get well with just token care, or they'll require a neurosurgeon, which I am not. Nobody can do anything out here. I'm just the guy who decides that whatever happens, you and I will keep the law off the broad because putting the law to the broad would serve no purpose in this case."

"Do you mean to say that, if these men died, you'd protect that woman?"

"Sure. Even if it got to court, no jury would convict her. So why let it get to court? Think of the taxpayers' money that would be saved."

"I believe your attitude is basically antisocial, Dr. Pierce. Society has certain rules, and if these rules are broken, we have no society."

"Think peripherally all you want," said Hawkeye. "Around here I'm known and you aren't so nobody'll pay any attention, even if you blow the whistle. What you ought to do is pursue this case, at the purely academic level. I'll bet you both these guys get a roll in the hay from this broad within a week after they're out of the hospital."

As Dr. Pierce and Professor Russell arrived at the hospital and helped unload Ben and John Simmons onto stretchers, Goofus MacDuff approached and said, "Hey, Hawkeye, they've been looking for you. The coast guard sent a plane out."

"Goofus, you don't mean it? My popularity knows no bounds. Are you going to tell me why the coast guard sent a plane out or are you just going to hint around?"

"Gee, they got a man with a flag in his chest. Everybody thought you should see him."

"I'll sure as hell go along with that, Goofus. Even a thoracic surgeon with my background and experience hardly ever gets to see a man with a flag in his chest. I'm some damn glad you thought of me."

"He's in the emergency room," said Goofus. "Trapper John is there."

Trapper John, called on the hospital-to-Thief-Island-Radio, had arrived ten minutes earlier and found that the patient, Reverend Titcomb of Tedium Cove, did indeed have a flag in his chest, the kind of flag sold everywhere durińg patriotic holidays. A small flag with a fairly firm, two-foot-long wooden staff, about two inches of which had penetrated the area between Reverend Titcomb's left fourth and fifth ribs, a little to the left of the breastbone. Trapper John, after one look at the patient, whose pulse and blood pressure were quite normal, realized that the flagstaff had penetrated the intercostal space, not damaged the heart, and that the wound, however impressive to onlookers, was inconsequential. Treatment would consist of removing the flag, applying a small dressing, injecting tetanus toxoid and perhaps an antibiotic. A day or two of hospitalization would be necessary to calm the patient's nerves.

Trapper, in swimming trunks, was accompanied by Lucinda Lively, in her usual bikini. Trapper, interrupted on a day of leisure may or may not have had a touch or two of Old Bejoyfull. Either way, Hawkeye knew that Trapper was putting on a show.

"What's the word, Trapper?" asked Hawkeye.

"Not my line of work. Apparently the guy's a vampire and somebody tried to drive a stake through his heart. He missed the heart. I got no use for vampires and if the heart is not involved, it's out of my field."

"The only thing in your field is cranberries," said Hawkeye. "Are you sure he's a vampire?"

"All I know is the stake isn't in his heart. Why don't you order a vampire test?"

Turning to Goofus MacDuff, who lurked in the background, Hawkeye ordered: "Goofus, you're the Medical Director. Unleash all your forces and find out if this guy is a vampire. Remove his right great toenail, soak it in Formalin for ten minutes and hold it up to the sun."

"What'll that prove?" asked Goofus.

"I don't know, but it might save your eyesight if there's an eclipse."

Hawkeye had been aware of Jocko Allcock's presence and had no doubt that Jocko would provide the basic facts of the case. Joining Jocko, he asked, "Well, who stuck the flag in Reverend Titcomb, and why?"

Jocko was only too pleased to supply the information. "The Reverend was over to Eagle Head this mornin' marriage counselin' Sally Witham. He was amarriage counselin' the livin' bejeezus out of her in that tent they got in their backyard when Jake come home. Seems like the old Chevy engine in his lobster boat blew somethin' and instead of haulin' off'n Egg Rock, he was to home. Jake ain't got nawthin' agin religion but he don't hold with marriage counselin'. He picked up that little flag was stuck in the lawn for the Fourth of July and he druv her right into the Reverend's chest."

"A true patriot," observed Hawkeye.

"Ayuh. I guess so," agreed Jocko.

A nurse approached and said: "Dr. McIntyre has turned the case over to you, Dr. Pierce."

Dr. Pierce went to see his new patient and introduced himself. "The Lord is my shepherd," the patient stated.

"Well, now, Reverend," said Hawkeye, "I'm reminded of a scene from *Mr. Roberts* in which a sailor, stricken with gonorrhea in a supposedly clapless area, sought treatment from his physician. His physician, quite logically under the circumstances, questioned the patient's basic philosophy, and withheld treatment until he'd made the patient fully aware of the significance of his affliction. I can do no less. You, Reverend, on the day after the Fourth of July, have our flag stuck in your chest. I understand your emotional discomfort but, after all, you are the only guy in Maine with a flag in your chest. I'll remove it, if you wish, but I want to be very sure that in the future you won't regret your decision."

"The Lord is my shepherd," answered Reverend Titcomb.

"Just in case Trapper's wrong, will someone move the Stars and Stripes about halfway down before I pull them out?" asked Hawkeye.

"What?" asked a nurse.

"That's the usual response to a simple order around

here," said Hawkeye. "Jocko, will you provide us with background music?"

"Oh say can you see, by the dawn's early light," sang Jocko, as Hawkeye pulled the flag from Reverend Titcomb's chest.

There was no gush of blood but suddenly, from afar, came the sounds of altercation. A nurse appeared, yelling: "There's a fight in the intensive-care unit."

"Ben and John have come to," said Hawkeye. "Jocko, why don't you take them home? Maybe the Professor will take me back to my boat."

Jim Russell drove Hawkeye to Tedium Cove. "How'd it grab you, Professor?" asked Hawkeye.

"I just don't know," said Professor Russell.

"I figured as much," said Hawkeye.

12

As summer progressed Trapper John and Lucinda prepared for a long life on Thief Island. Trapper bought a twenty-six-foot diesel-powered lobster boat. A wooden floor appeared in The Swamp, as well as insulation and two potbellied oil stoves—one more than in the original, Korean Swamp. Lucinda, a lover of animals, had acquired, with no encouragement from Trapper, a Saint Bernard puppy, a black sheep, a white sheep and a pony.

In late July, Hawkeye Pierce, no longer on vacation, had lunch with Lucinda at the Bay View Café while Trapper fussed the postoperative care of a cardiac case. This was, in fact, Hawkeye's first private meeting with his former secretary since the arrival of Trapper John.

"How is it?" asked Hawkeye.

"Beautiful. I've fallen in love with the guy, hook, line and sinker."

"I'm glad," said Hawkeye. "When are you getting married?"

Lucinda looked down at her beer and a common vascular phenomenon intensified the pink of her sunburned face. "I guess I touched a nerve," said Hawkeye.

"Yes, Trapper wants to wait a year."

"And you don't?"

"No, I want to have a baby and get married. I also want a goat."

"In that order?" asked Hawk.

"Any order."

"I won't bother to ask about the goat. No wonder Trapper wants to wait a year. Christ, if I had a broad who wanted a goat, I'd wait a year, too. Why don't you get pregnant and force his hand?"

"He won't let me."

"How in hell have you avoided it? I know as your former doctor that you can't take the pill and your periods are irregular as hell. What do you mean, he won't let you?"

"Well, we sort of play Pope's pinball and he takes my temperature every morning. He says if it's over ninety-nine it means I'm ovulating and he rests for a few days."

"I'll take care of that," Hawkeye said.

Between cases the next morning Hawkeye gave Lucinda Lively a thermometer.

"What's this?" asked Lucinda.

"It's a very special thermometer," Hawkeye told her.

"How so?"

"Babe, it's locked in at 98.6 degrees. It can't go up."

Hawkeye was confident that he'd solved Lucinda's problem and that the solution needed no embellishment. Two days later, however, the Reverend Richard Titcomb, his flag-dented thorax nearly healed, appeared in Hawk's office for a final checkup. Reassured about his health, the Reverend expounded his newly discovered divine mission, which was to forsake all sin, particularly of the flesh, and to rescue others weakened by lust.

"Amen," said Dr. Pierce. "Such a sinner is Dr. McIntyre of Thief Island. Reverend Titcomb, I beg you, save him."

The Reverend Titcomb responded appropriately. He charged out of Hawkeye's officc suffused with zeal and godliness. No one aware of his mission could doubt that Trapper and Lucinda would soon be shown the path of righteousness.

Dr. Pierce, as soon as Reverend Titcomb left, leaned back in his chair and laughed his head off. He had visions of the Reverend invading the cranberry bog; of the Reverend finding Trapper and Lucinda in a moment of passion; of Trapper John hurling the Reverend into the ocean. Dr. Pierce imagined all kinds of ridiculous happenings, but his imagination was meager and uninspired. He could not possibly guess that because he gave Reverend Titcomb a mission Pasquale Merlino would, while hauling in a seine full of herring, get hit on the head by a mackerel.

Two days later Lucinda Lively described to Hawkeye the Reverend Titcomb's visit to Thief Island.

Much to her surprise, Trapper John had not rejected Mr. Titcomb. He had listened, humbly, to the Reverend's exhortation. He had knelt in prayer with Reverend Titcomb on the newly installed wooden floor of The Swamp. Lucinda was quite impressed. Also she was worried.

"It just doesn't seem normal for Trapper," she said.

"It isn't," Hawk said. "I touted Titcomb onto Trapper for a laugh. It won't make any difference. Just use my thermometer. We'll both have to wait and see what Trapper's up to."

As an undergraduate Dr. McIntyre had been an enthusiastic member of the Dartmouth Outing Club. While serving as an army surgeon in Korea he had learned to fly helicopters. He intended secretly to fly to the top of Mount Everest and implant the banner of the Dartmouuth Outing Club where it could be discovered by Sir Edmund Hillary, or whoever got there second. A variety of technical, financial and other problems had frustrated this ambition, so he'd settled for burning down the officers' latrine.

Hawkeye believed that a man with this kind of vision and resourcefulness could cope with the Reverend Richard Titcomb. He heard, the day after the Reverend's visit to Thief Island, that Trapper John was buying beer for Wrong Way Napolitano in the Bay View Café and knew that something would happen soon.

After the first beer, Wrong Way had said: "If you and Lucinda are looking for a raise, forget it. Intercontinental will pay one hundred a week and no more."

"Such a thought never entered my mind," Trapper assured him. "I understand you have great reflexes."

"This is true," admitted Wrong Way.

"Excellent," said Trapper. "I want you to acquire a new skill."

"Such as?"

"I want you to learn how to stick a fish in a guy's ear from an altitude of one thousand feet."

To a lesser man than Wrong Way Napolitano this statement might have seemed, at best, bizarre. Wrong Way was not the common, ordinary man. "This is a true challenge," he said. "Whose ear?"

"The Reverend Titcomb's."

"What type fish did you have in mind?"

"You will need pinpoint accuracy with everything from sardines to halibut. Also loaves of bread."

"Loaves of bread?" asked Wrong Way.

"Yeah."

"It's a detail and not important, and I don't want to seem unduly curious, or nosy, and it's none of my business but—"

"You mean you want to know why you are to stick a fish in the Reverend's ear?" asked Trapper.

"I admit to a certain curiosity."

"Sticking one in his ear is but a figure of speech. I do, however, want him blessed with fish and bread at a time and in a place which I shall select. The Reverend Titcomb is an unusual human being, perhaps even more than human. I believe he has star quality."

"No doubt about it," agreed Wrong Way. "Biggest skin baron in the State of Maine. Present company excepted, of course."

"I am interested in developing a different facet of his character. I believe that he has star quality as a theologian and that all he needs is that one big break, which I am going to provide. I believe that the world, not Tedium Cove, is his parish."

Wrong Way took a long pull at his beer, achieved a look of deep reflection, and said, "I got a feeling that this conversation is getting nowhere. What exactly do you want me to do?"

"You fish-spotting tonight?"

"Yes."

"Good," said Trapper. "Just take me along. I'll bring a few mackerel and you can start working out. Can we take that plane you use for the parachute jumpers? You'll need to lean out and wind up if you're going to get the right action on the fish."

That evening Trapper appeared at Spruce Harbor International Jetport with a bushel basket of mackerel which he and Lucinda had caught from the shore of Thief Island, just north of the cranberry bog. Out over the bay Trapper took the controls while Wrong Way threw mackerel after mackerel at the boats below. The bushel basket was nearly empty before he got the hang of it. Unloading the one hundred and third mackerel, he watched its course for a moment and yelled: "Trapper! Look. That one's on target all the way."

Trapper looked down and saw Pasquale Merlino stagger, put his hands to his head and then, in obvious consternation, look to the heavens. "I guess that's enough for tonight," Trapper said.

Darkness came. The aviators and the fishermen returned to port and congregated in the Bay View Café. Pasquale Merlino told an enthralled audience how he'd been hit on the head by a mackerel.

"I'm a thinka it's a sign," said Pasquale after his fourth beer. "Maybe I'm a gonna be da nexta Pope."

Trapper John and Wrong Way decided to eschew live targets and, for a week, they practiced hitting Thrumbcap Ledge with various fish and loaves of bread. Wrong Way, possessed of great reflexes, was intrigued by this endeavor and did, indeed, achieve nearly pinpoint accuracy. Having honed their technique on Thrumbcap, they concentrated on other targets, including the Tedium Cove Church and the Finestkind Clinic and Fishmarket. The presence of mackerel in both areas was attributed, by the public, to seagulls.

Lucinda Lively called on Hawkeye at his office one afternoon, after the last patient had left. Fully dressed for once, she sat nervously in Hawk's consulting room.

"What's up, babe?" asked Dr. Pierce.

"Trapper has proposed. We are getting married on Sunday, September twenty-eighth, the day the clinic opens."

"Finestkind," said Hawkeye.

"I'm not so sure."

"Why?"

"That idiot, Titcomb, came out to the island again," she said, "and he and Trapper must have prayed for twenty minutes and then Trapper announced that we would get married on September twenty-eighth."

"So what's the problem? Isn't that what you want?"

"It's just so screwy. Now Trapper says that Reverend Titcomb is going to deliver the invocation when the clinic opens and then marry us a couple hours later in Me Lay's back yard. I don't want anything to do with that nut."

Hawkeye laughed. "Sounds to me," he said, "as though Trapper has really heard the word."

"Oh, please, Hawk. I don't want to marry a nut. What is going on?"

"Let's have a drink," said Hawk. "Let me find the office jug and some ice and I'll explain the fundamentals of this even though I don't know the details."

Lucinda drained half her drink in a gulp and said: "So explain."

"Look, honey. Trapper was probably about to propose to you anyhow. Then came Titcomb. Trapper is a guy who likes to do everything in a peculiar way. He is making a project of Titcomb and your imminent marriage is a byproduct of Trapper's project."

"Good lord," wailed Lucinda, "you mean my wedding is going to be the byproduct of a project?"

"Oh, for Chrissake, take it easy. You love him. He wouldn't marry you if he didn't love you. He just has a project. Will you deny him that? Can I have my thermometer back, now that you are engaged?"

"I should say not. I still intend to have my baby."

"And your goat?"

"Of course."

The tide was high in Crabapple Cove at 7 P.M. on the hot evening of September 18, and the Pierce family was having a cookout in their back yard. The noise and dissension which normally accompanies a cookout involving young children was intruded upon by the sound of a boat's horn. Looking due east the Pierces saw a boat coming full tilt, its horn blowing repeatedly.

"Who in hell is that?" asked Hawkeye.

"It's Uncle Trapper and Aunt Lucinda," said a young Pierce.

"Wonder why they're coming here?" Mary Pierce asked her husband. "I thought they never did anything but have sexual intercourse."

"Perhaps Aunt Lucinda has become frigid and Trapper is coming for *you.*"

"I doubt it," said Mary, "but I can dream until they get here."

The new lobster boat charged into Hawkeye's inlet and bumped into his wharf. Trapper and Lucinda jumped out, threw a line to Billy Pierce, and ran up the lawn.

"Hawkeye, Hawkeye," yelled Trapper.

"What the Christ ails you?" demanded Hawk.

"We're gonna have a kid," proclaimed Trapper John.

"Oh, I'm so happy," said Mary to Lucinda, who was now in tears.

"I love the broad," announced Trapper.

"That'll turn out to be handy as time goes by," Hawkeye observed. "I gather we are the first to know?"

"Sure."

"It would be within the realm of reason to allow the news to stop here, would it not? I mean, usually this type news is dispensed after the wedding."

"I came for booze and congratulations, not sociology. Gimme a drink," demanded Trapper John, "and send one of the kids down to Lew the Jew's and tell him he's going to be best man at the wedding."

Sunday, September 28, dawned like so many dawns on the rockbound coast of Maine. There was fog and a steady, relentless drizzle which occasionally became rain. It was in Dr. and Mrs. Me Lay Marston's spacious back yard, no more than a drive and a five iron from Thief Island, that Trapper and Lucinda were to be married. Me Lay and Mrs. Marston were unhappy about the weather. They called Maria Tannenbaum, who called Tip Toe at Idlewild and soon a message came: the sun will shine on Trapper and Lucinda and on the grand opening of the Finestkind Clinic and Fishmarket.

Dr. Pierce, bothering everybody, had planned on missing the grand opening and playing golf. He stubbornly insisted that all the clinic needed was to open and that ceremonies were unnecessary. Whatever the weather authorities at Idlewild said about the afternoon, even Hawkeye rejected morning golf in the fog and rain. He made rounds in the new Spruce Harbor General, found everyone reasonably healthy and decided to inspect Wooden Leg's new wharf, separated by a wide lawn from the Finestkind Clinic and Fishmarket. Parked at the wharf was a jeep which, he knew, belonged to Wrong Way Napolitano.

Inside the fish palace, Hawkeye found Wrong Way cursing and struggling with a halibut which must have weighed at least a hundred pounds. Every time the aviator seemed to get a stranglehold on it, the huge fish would slip to the floor.

"How long you been stealin' fish?" Hawk inquired.

"You got it all wrong," protested Wrong Way. "This is not larceny. It's an act of God. Leastways it will be if I can get this and that other one over there into the jeep. You wanta help?"

"Such an opportunity comes even less than once in some lifetimes. I would consider it a rare privilege."

"Okay," said Wrong Way after the purloined fish were safely in the jeep. "Meet me at the airport. I may need a little help delivering these things. Some acts of God require group effort."

Wooden Leg Wilcox arrived just in time to see Wrong Way's jeep leaving the premises. Discovering the loss of two halibut which the Massasoit Inn had specifically ordered for this Sunday, Leg put two and two together and raced for the airport. Hawkeye and Wrong Way, having loaded the halibut aboard, were just climbing into the plane when Wooden Leg pulled up in his pickup truck, and demanded, "Gimme back my halibut, you guinea bastard."

"Can't do it, Leg. Don't worry. You'll receive your recompense in heaven." With that, Wrong Way taxied to the runway and took off.

Airborne, Hawkeye inspected the other cargo and found five loaves of Double-Enriched Superbread (builds strong bodies twelve ways). "What's the bread for?" he asked.

"I don't know. The customer ordered two fish and five loaves."

The visibility was limited, and Hawkeye was uneasy while Wrong Way searched the gloom for Eagle Head Light. He found it and banked sharply to starboard, barely missing it. Circling around he said: "We start our run at 10:52. I'll take care of the loaves. When I give the word, dump those halibut."

"What are we trying to destroy?" asked Hawkeye.

"Nothing. Don't worry. Trapper and I got it down to a fine art."

"Have you worked with halibut before?"

"No, but I thought it would be a nice touch."

"Jesus, you *are* a crazy guinea. We're likely to wipe out half of Spruce Harbor with these goddamn halibut."

"Quiet," growled Wrong Way. "We're about to start our run."

"Hey, Wrong Way, I hear a team of Italian surgeons just performed the first successful hernia transplant."

"What?"

While Wrong Way and Hawkeye roamed the still cloudy but clearing sky in a halibut laden Tri-Pacer, a crowd gathered for the grand opening of the Finestkind Clinic and Fishmarket. Community leaders from Spruce Harbor and adjoining towns were proud to attend. Hospital administrators and physicians from all over Maine had made the pilgrimage. Nurses and paramedical personnel abounded. Representatives of the fishing industry included Pasquale Merlino and Zeke Simmons. Duke Forrest, Tony Holcombe, Spearchucker Jones were there with their families. Mary Pierce, resigned to her husband's peculiar ways, arrived with Billy and Steve Pierce. Several high-ranking members of the Cardia Nostra, former colleagues of Trapper John's, managed to get there, slightly obtunded by prenuptial ceremonies held the previous evening. Trapper and Lucinda, of course, were there.

At 11 A.M., while Wooden Leg Wilcox leaned against the railing on his new wharf and absent-mindedly stabbed his right thigh with an ice pick, Dr. Goofus MacDuff, Medical Director (by acclamation) of the Finestkind Clinic, introduced the guest speaker, Dr. Maxwell Neville of Saint Lombard's Hospital. Dr. Neville, by now, had recovered from his flight from New York the day before with Wrong Way Napolitano, who had dropped five mackerel in the vicinity of home plate while flying over Fenway Park.

Maxie Neville praised the ambition, the foresight, the determination of the men who were bringing advanced surgical and medical skills to Spruce Harbor. His talk was brief, straightforward, to the point and easily quoted by the *Spruce Harbor Courier*. Most important, his endorsement established Trapper John as the don of Spruce Harbor—a man whose work in cardiovascular surgery should receive continued subsidization from charitable foundations and goverment agencies.

At 11:20 Dr. MacDuff thanked Dr. Neville and introduced the Reverend Richard Titcomb who, he proclaimed rather dubiously, would deliver the invocation. Reverend Titcomb moved with alacrity and zest into his talk. At 11:25, Trapper John, at the rear of the crowd, raised his right arm as the Reverend said, "And they say unto Him, we have here but five loaves and two fishes.

"He said, bring them hither to me," continued Reverend Titcomb and was about to add: "and he commanded the multitude to sit down upon the grass" when the Finestkind Clinic and Fishmarket took two direct hits. Each fish landed on the roof with a loud, frightening bang and then, on the first bounce, at the feet of Reverend Richard Titcomb.

The crowd, stunned, barely noticed five loaves of bread which, with one exception, floated harmlessly down upon them. One loaf of Double-Enriched Superbread struck Lew Pierce on the right shoulder, causing him to exclaim: "Shit a goddamn."

Among the first to assess the situation was Zeke Simmons. "By the Jesus," observed Zeke, "I guess someone sure'n hell brung them hither to him. The Lord heard that young feller. Tain't often we get a parson like that around heah."

"It's a miracle. A message from the Lord," avowed Trapper John, genuflecting before Reverend Titcomb, while local TV cameras recorded the event.

"Why don't you kiss his feet while you're at it?" asked Lucinda Lively.

As the crowd, fear and surprise overcome, began to comprehend what had befallen, they surged around Reverend Titcomb. "Hallelujah," stated several elderly ladies.

"Didn't I tell you he's divine," said one young matron to another.

Mrs. Ophelia Witherspoon of the *Spruce Harbor Courier*, after thirty years of covering the Eastern Star, church meetings and baked-bean suppers, knew her time had come. Within five minutes she was on the phone to everywhere and an hour later radio stations throughout New England and the world were supplying their listeners with early, still fragmentary details of The Miracle of Spruce Harbor.

Jocko Allcock, informed in advance of The Miracle, had appointed himself Reverend Titcomb's business manager and press secretary. He had rented a suite at the Massasoit Inn where, between The Miracle and the wedding, the Reverend could remain incommunicado and where, after the wedding, he could receive the press.

And so it came to pass that the Reverend Titcomb even after the sun came out on this glorious day, was slow to understand how brightly the Lord had made his face to shine upon him. Bemused, confused, that afternoon, he joined Trapper John McIntyre and Lucinda Lively in some kind of matrimony.

At the wedding, Hawkeye provided the only offbeat note by arriving with a goat, which he led on a leash.

"Good-looking goat," said Trapper.

"Glad you like him," said Hawkeye. "He's yours."

"Oh Hawkeye!" said Lucinda, kissing him.

"Oh, Jesus," said Trapper.

"Son of a howah," observed the best man, Mr. Lewis Pierce.

At the reception, where Me Lay provided more than enough of everything, the happy couple divulged that their honeymoon would be spent on Thief Island. Many well-wishers seemed to feel that this had been used up as a honeymoon spot. Trapper patiently explained that when you live on a place like Thief Island there's really no other place to go because you're already there.

Three days later Intercontinental's flight from Rome landed at Spruce Harbor to pick up lobsters and ten members of the international press. They were accompanying the Reverend Richard Titcomb and his manager, Mr. Jocko Allcock, who were embarking on the first leg of a worldwide crusade.

As Captain Tannenbaum took off from Spruce Harbor International Jetport, he announced over the intercom: "Ladies and gentlemen, the ancient Indian fertility rites on Thief Island, which our passengers have been privileged to view for the past three months, have been canceled because of cold weather. However, if you look down you can see the happy couple, their home, their domestic animals, including a goat, and the famous cranberry bog."

Trapper and Lucinda, sensibly dressed, stood next to the cranberry bog and waved at the plane. In the pilot's cabin, Captain Tannenbaum said to his copilot, "Looks like they got a sheet over the cranberries with something written on it. What's it say?"

Wrong Way Napolitano studied the area with binoculars and replied: "Hey, Tip Toe, it says FINESTKIND."

13

The first year of the Finestkind Clinic and Fishmarket was a success. Its founders felt that their vision and ambition had been justified and that they had created a rural medical center which rivaled and, in certain ways, surpassed the big city competition. In the Finestkind Clinic and in the Spruce Harbor General Hospital, patients were made to feel important, and patients like this.

The cardiovascular surgical unit flourished and

Trapper gradually reintroduced Hawkeye Pierce to the Cardia Nostra. Lucinda Lively gave birth to a son. The surgeons were busy and thinking about bringing in new talent. There was, however, no real excitement until shortly after the 1960 presidential election when Coot Yeaton's jackass got the colic. Coot, an amoral, alcoholic, indigent seventy-year-old former rum-runner, had not been gainfully employed since the repeal of the Volstead Act. When out of jail, Coot had a succession of housekeepers who shared his shack on a lonely cove on the north end of East Haven Island, but his true love was George, a big gray jackass. George and Coot were inseparable. On the rare days when Coot decided to tend his lobster traps George came right along in Coot's old lobster boat. On windy summer days, people in pleasure boats would see, in the distance, a jackass walking on water. Even when they closed in for a better look there seemed to be more jackass than boat. Coot made as much money posing with George as he made hauling lobsters. The pleasure cruisers had to have pictures to prove to themselves that they hadn't been drunk and hallucinating.

Three days after the election of John F. Kennedy, Coot and George, with George jumping, kicking, and braying, charged into Wooden Leg's wharf, just below the Finestkind Clinic. Coot jumped out and tied up. Goerge jumped out and kicked his heels and threatened everything in sight.

"You get that christly jackass the hell off my wharf, you crazy old bastard," yelled Wooden Leg.

"I gotta git George to Doggy Moore. He's got the colic."

"Oh, my sweet holy Jesus," exclaimed Wooden Leg. "I gotta see this. Stick that jack in the back of my truck. I'll take you to the emergency room."

At the emergency room, Coot Yeaton ran in and demanded: "Git Doggy. My ahss is sick."

"We'll call Dr. Moore, sir," the nurse assured him. "May I ask you a few questions?"

"Showah," agreed Coot. "Whatcha wanta know?"

"May I have your name and address?"

"Whatcha want that for? I ain't sick. It's my ahss is sick. George."

"What?" asked the nurse.

"George," repeated Coot. "My ahss. He's sicker'n hell. Prob'ly got the christly colic."

One can only speculate about where this conversation might have led had not Dr. Doggy Moore and Mr. Wooden Leg Wilcox arrived simultaneously.

"Coot," said Wooden Leg, "your ahss is kickin' the shit out of my truck. Hurry up and get him a bed, will yuh?"

"Coot," said Doggy Moore, "did you bring that colicky jack in here again?"

"Damn it, Doggy, you told me not to bring him to your office no more. You said bring him to the hospital. That's what I done."

Doggy, with his years of experience, didn't argue with Coot or bother to point out, as younger men might have, that he was not a jackass doctor.

"George got insurance yet, Coot?" Doggy asked. "I am tired of treating him for nothing."

"I could let you have some lobsters. Just take care of George. Please, Doggy."

"I'll see what I can do."

Soon after George began to respond to an enema, which Doggy administered with the help of a garden hose, a northeaster blew up, making the return trip to East Haven impossible for Coot and George. George was given a private room at Wooden Leg's wharf and Coot, knowing no other recreation, headed for the Bay

View Café. Hawkeye, aware of what had happened, sent word to his uncle, Lew the Jew Pierce, that Coot could use company. Coot and Lew were old friends, so Lew mounted his Cadillac and drove to Spruce Harbor.

By midevening Coot and Lew the Jew had made significant progress. They relived the days when they'd run booze from Saint Pierre and Miquelon in a schooner named *Sarah Pierce* after Lew's wife, who'd died in childbirth. They fascinated the customers with the tale of the schooner, heavy with Cutty Sark, hitting an iceberg in the Gulf of Saint Lawrence and four days later leaving a Coast Guard cutter hung up on Thrumbcap Ledge while they slipped, in darkness, into Otter Island Cove.

Reminiscences over, their conversation turned to politics. This had always been a sensitive subject with Lew Pierce, a lifelong Republican who, even in 1960, felt that, as menaces to society, mad dogs and Democrats were neck and neck. Lew, although aware that his friend Coot was eccentric, was not prepared for Coot's statement: "By the Jesus, Jew. I done somethin' I never done afoah. I voted the straight Democratic ticket. Son of a howah."

"Son of a howah," agreed Lew the Jew, too overwrought to think of a more poignant comment.

At this point in the political dialogue Doggy Moore arrived at the Bay View to discuss, with Bette Bang-Bang, Mattress Mary and Made Marion, a particularly virulent strain of *Neisseria gonococcus*. This organism, resistant to the usual antibiotics, had so curtailed the girls' business that for three days their only customer had been Half A Man Timberlake. Even Half A Man—who, according to Dr. Moore, was immune to venereal disease—was slacking off from plain old fatigue, a previously unrecorded phenomenon. Doggy, having obtained cultures and antibiotic sensitivity tests on the girls, arrived with a new oral antibiotic, which he hoped would make them sweet and clean. He recalled the exhortations, two days earlier, of Wooden Leg Wilcox, who had said: "Chrissake, Doggy, if you don't clean up them howahs, the President's gonna have to declare Spruce Harbor a disaster area."

While Dr. Moore gave meticulous instructions to Bette, Mary and Marion, Lew the Jew and Coot Yeaton stood at the bar and continued their political debate. With very few preliminaries, the debate dwindled to invective. For example, Mr. Lewis Pierce made this statement: "Democrats sleep with snakes, run rabbits, bark at the moon and they get so jeezly tired they gotta pay somebody to go pick up their relief check. By the Jesus, Coot, I got a mind to muckle onto you."

"You ain't got no call to be so nasty," wailed Coot. "And you better not muckle onto me, if'n you know what's good for yuh. I guess not, by the old Billy Bejeezus."

"If'n I was to muckle onto you," declared Mr. Lewis Pierce, "I'd throw you fifteen, maybe twenty foot, fust time I took aholt."

Ace Kimball, the bartender, had been monitoring the Great Pierce–Yeaton Debate. Ace felt that the situation was deteriorating so he reached for the forty-five pistol he kept behind the bar for riot control. He was prepared to shoot at a two-foot-square area in the ceiling which was specially reinforced for just this purpose. One shot had always quelled violence in the Bay View Café.

It all happened very quickly. Lew the Jew muckled onto Coot. Doggy Moore, too late, left the booth he shared with his patients, hoping to intercede. Ace Kimball tried to get off a shot at the ceiling, just as Coot

Yeaton, in orbit over the bar, hit his right shoulder Ace missed the ceiling and shot Doggy Moore in the chest.

Doggy fell in his tracks, was momentarily stunned, but within seconds he took full command. "Call Trapper John," he ordered Ace. "He'll call Hawkeye and Duke. Do that first, so they'll be on their way. Then call the ambulance. Then call the emergency room and let me talk to whoever's on duty."

After getting Trapper and the ambulance, Ace called the emergency room and held the phone for Doggy who said: "This here's Doggy. I been shot. I want a dozen pints of blood. I gotta be operated on tonight. Get Me Lay. The other fellers are on their way."

The local police arrived just as Doggy was being placed on a stretcher by the ambulance crew, all of whom were more nervous and scared than usual because they'd all been delivered by Doggy Moore.

"What happened, Doggy? Can you gimme a statement?" asked the Chief of Police.

"It was an accident. No one to blame. Don't arrest anybody for this."

Doggy Moore then became unconscious, because, as it turned out, there was a small hole in the apex of the left ventricle of his heart. Every time his heart beat, blood was forced out through this tiny hole into the pericardium, the membrane which contains the heart.

Lucinda Lively and Trapper John were waiting when the ambulance arrived. Trapper ordered an immediate chest X-ray, inspected the wound, and took Doggy's blood pressure, which was 80/65.

"I don't need to see the X-ray," he said. "Get the pump ready, hon. We may need it."

In the year since her marriage, Lucinda had become

Trapper's cardiac bypass expert. Progress was such that, instead of the horde of Filipinos which Big Charley in Philly had employed a few years earlier, one bright blond could run an effective, if unsophisticated, extracorporeal pump, a machine which, for short periods, did the work of the heart.

Duke and Hawkeye arrived just as Trapper got the first pint of blood running into Doggy and was exposing a vein in his groin to start another.

"What's the score?" asked Duke.

"It hit his heart. He's bleeding into his pericardium. I figure we go as soon as the OR is set up. Me Lay's here. We can't screw around with this one."

"What else is hit?" asked Duke.

"Christ only knows," said Hawkeye, inspecting the hole in Doggy's back from which the bullet emerged. "There's lots of things it could have hit, but the heart's the word for now. Let's fix that, load him with antibiotics and bide our time. He can't stand a whole night of surgery. Either way, though, we'd better check his spleen."

"Right," said Trapper.

At this stage of the game there was no apparent need for Dr. Spearchucker Jones but he appeared in the dressing room as the other surgeons changed into scrub clothes. He changed, too, saying: "I'll just be handy, in case one of you guys faints from the sight of blood."

"Anybody got a butt?" asked Trapper.

"I thought you'd quit," said Hawkeye.

"I want a butt," insisted Trapper.

Spearchucker found cigarettes and they all smoked.

"Just like MASH all over again," said Hawk.

A few minutes later, while Lucinda stood ready to run the pump if the need arose, Trapper made an incision between the left fourth and fifth ribs, cut across the breastbone, and extended the incision between the same ribs on the right. He put in a big retractor, turned its handle and the membrane which surrounded the heart, bulging, obviously full of blood, protruded into the wound.

"You gonna stick him on the pump?" asked Duke.

"Shut the hell up. Honey," he said to the nurse, "have 2-0 silk sutures ready—those swedged on jobs."

"I figure it's just one hole," Trapper explained, "maybe two, but we should be able to control the bleeding long enough to close them."

Trapper opened the membrane and blood gushed out. Trapper scooped clot with his hands. At the apex of the ventricle, where the bullet had grazed the heart, there was one small hole. Two stitches closed it.

Everyone sighed. "The spleen," said Hawkeye. "Open the diaphragm."

"Yeah," said Trapper.

The spleen was bleeding merrily.

"Rip it," said Hawk.

"Yeah."

A three-minute splenectomy was followed by a hasty inspection of the area, which revealed no obvious damage to the other organs. At the end of the procedure, Doggy's blood pressure was 100/60, and all seemed well.

"You guys still have it," said Me Lay. "Good job."

"We haven't heard the last of this one," said Duke.

"No," Hawk agreed, "but we can handle the rest of it on our terms, not the bullet's."

Doggy Moore was taken from the OR to the intensive-care unit with a catheter in his bladder, a tube through his nose leading to his stomach, a tube coming out of each side of his chest and emptying into separate bottles, partly filled with water, and with two blood transfusions running. Two hours later when he regained consciousness, Doggy assessed his situation and asked a nurse: "Whatsamatter, honey? Can't you find something to stick in my ear?"

The surgeons did not leave the hospital that night. With the exception of Spearchucker, they all canceled the next day's surgery. "I ain't doin' nothin'," proclaimed Duke, "till that Yankee doctor is out of the woods. Besides, he's got blood in his urine. You guys maybe don't know it but I saw Doggy a year ago because of some kidney trouble. His right kidney isn't the best and I figure he's shot in the left one. We gotta try to save it."

"You got any other good news?" asked Me Lay.

"Let's get some sleep," suggested Hawkeye.

At 7:30 A.M. the surgeons, unshaven, unwashed, sleepy, entered the intensive-care unit. They'd said nothing to each other. They were nervous. The night before they'd had the adrenalin running but now they feared a variety of complications. Secretly, each knew that being objective about this particular patient would require a great and willful effort. To each came the thought: Let's unload him, send him to Boston. And, to each came a second thought: No, by Jesus, we can't trust those bastards. We'll take care of him.

Of the six patients in the intensive-care unit, two belonged to Doggy Moore. The surgeons found their patient sitting on the edge of his bed, writing orders on a chart. Their patient was saying to the patient in the next bed, "Goddamn it, Rufus, you don't get out of bed till I tell you to. You hear me?"

"Sure, I guesso, if you say so, Doggy," agreed Rufus.

"How they goin', Doggy?" Hawk asked, sort of timidly.

"I got blood in my urine," said Doggy.

"Considering the broads you were out with last night, you could have worse than that in your urine," said Hawkeye. "Wait'll I tell Emma."

"We're gonna watch the urine, and we're gonna X-ray your kidneys, Doggy," Duke explained. "If worst comes to worst, we'll have a look at that left kidney but I don't want to whack it all out. If you'll bother to remember, your right one ain't a winner."

"I remember," said Doggy. "What else?"

"Well," said Hawk. "Your left lung caught a little but that's no problem. Also stomach, colon, even small bowel were potentially in the line of fire. We didn't take time to look carefully. We just let Trapper fix the hole in your heart and called it a night, except for grabbing your spleen."

"I can tell," said Doggy. "I'm the picture of health."

The surgeons consulted, wrote orders and went to the Bay View Café for breakfast, which was a mistake. Even riding the two miles to the Bay View, they sensed something. Hawkeye was reminded of Moose Lord. Passing cars stopped and waved them down. "How's Doggy?" everyone asked.

"Okay for now, but keep your fingers crossed," was the answer they kept repeating.

They found Wooden Leg Wilcox in the Bay View nursing a beer. Early in the day, even for Wooden Leg.

"Hey, Leg" asked Hawk, "where are Coot and the Jew?"

"I sent them both out to East Haven at five thirty, along with George before they got lynched."

"Good idea," agreed Hawkeye. "Maybe we oughta lynch George. If that jackass didn't get the colic every two weeks, life around here would be easier."

Reluctantly, the surgeons all appeared at their

offices that afternoon. At three o'clock Hawkeye received a call from the intensive-care unit.

"Dr. Pierce?"

"Yes."

"We wonder if Dr. Moore should be seeing patients. He's terribly tired."

"What the hell are you talking about?"

"Doggy is holding office hours in the intensive-care unit."

"I'll be there," said Hawkeye.

Half an hour later, Dr. Pierce, now shaven and washed, stalked into the room where Doggy was holding court, told everyone to get the hell out and gave Dr. Moore the word.

"Okay, Doggy. Trapper operated on your heart. Duke may have to work on your kidney. God knows what else may come of this. You get this through your thick skull right now. I am running the show. You are going to be a patient, not a doctor, and you and everybody else are going to do what I say. Right now I'm ordering one hundred milligrams of Demerol and I want you to lie in the weeds for a while. If you give me any bullshit, I'll ship your ass to Boston. Any questions?"

"Gawd," said Doggy, "you don't have to be so ugly."

"I'll be any way I have to be to get you well."

"Okay. Maybe I could use some rest."

That evening, before going home, Hawkeye and Trapper both checked Dr. Moore. This time he was asleep and breathing quietly. His pulse was slow and steady. As the surgeons left the hospital, they saw a strange group of people milling around on the lawn which separated the Spruce Harbor General from the Finestkind Clinic and Fishmarket.

"Hey, Hawkeye," said Trapper, "I think it's a

Pierce family reunion. Get a load of that bunch of grunts."

Hawkeye, in a glance, discovered that the smaller members of this group looked like chipmunks and the larger ones like muskrats. "They're more Doggy's family than mine," he told Trapper. "Those are the Finch-Browns."

"Are they in season?" asked Trapper.

"Always open season on them. Why don't you take one home to Lucinda. She likes pets."

Before Trapper could consider this suggestion, a large, graying muskrat, Elihu Finch-Brown, yelled, "Hey, Hawkeye."

"How they goin', Elihu?" Hawk inquired solicitously.

"Piss poah," asserted Elihu. "We come to be with Doggy."

"Elihu, I know Doggy will be pleased but he can't see anyone right now. In the morning I'll tell him you were here."

"I'll tell the rest of 'em to go home," said Elihu, "but me and Bessie is stayin' till Doggy gets well. We can sleep in the pickup."

"Okay, Elihu," said Hawkeye. "Send the rest of them home. I'll get a room for you and Bessie at the Spruce Harbor Motel."

"Nossuh," wailed Elihu. "We ain't never been to no motel."

"You're going to one, Elihu. Doggy'd want you to be near and comfortable."

Given the word from their leader, the chipmunks and muskrats evacuated the area and then Elihu and Bessie Finch-Brown, in their dilapidated pickup truck, followed Hawkeye and Trapper John to the Spruce Harbor Motel. Hawkeye discussed a few things with the management, led the guests to their room, explained the plumbing and TV set and left them so dazzled by the grandeur of their surroundings that, for a few minutes, they forgot their grief.

In the motel bar, Hawk and Trapper had a drink and Trapper said, "How do you explain this?"

"You've seen that plaque over the entrance to the pediatric ward, haven't you?"

"The one that says 'In Memory of C. Moore, Captain USAAF'?"

"Yeah."

"The C. stands for Chipmunk. Doggy raised him. He belonged to Bessie and Elihu. He went to college with me. He was a fighter pilot."

"I guess I'll have another drink," said Trapper John.

In the morning there was trouble. Dr. Moore's speech was slurred and his left arm and leg were weak. He was aware of his problem and explained that in recent months he'd had similar transient episodes, none this severe. He asked for Spearchucker Jones. His urine was, still, very bloody.

Dr. Jones said, very simply, "I think his right common carotid is blocked. I'm going to do an arteriogram and find out. The kidney can wait."

That afternoon, assisted by Hawkeye, Spearchucker did a carotid endarterectomy, that is, he reamed out deposits of fat and calcium which were blocking blood flow to the right side of Doggy's brain. Within twelve hours, Doggy regained normal speech and the use of his left side. In less than forty-eight hours, Dr. Moore had had two major operations.

Another morning came. When the surgeons visited their patient, he said, "I want a day off, but Duke, you plan on fixing that kidney tomorrow."

"Yes, Doggy, I guess that's a good idea," agreed Duke.

Enough time had gone by to suggest that the surgeons had not missed bullet holes in stomach, large bowel or small bowel and that all they had to do was fix the kidney. Duke did a heminephrectomy. He removed the lower third of the left kidney, which was destroyed, useless and bleeding, but was able to preserve the rest of the organ.

Doggy Moore's recovery from his third major operation in five days was, in a sense, quicker than the surgeons could logically hope for but slow enough to make them nervous. Emotionally they were as depleted as was Doggy physically.

Half the population of Spruce Harbor and the surrounding area seemed to hover around the hospital. Hawkeye kept visitors out of the intensive-care unit except for Emma Moore. Two days after the kidney surgery, Elihu and Bessie Finch-Brown were allowed to visit. No matter how hard he tried, though, Hawkeye couldn't protect the patient completely. A variety of emergencies, or seeming emergencies, arose with Doggy's patients. Various doctors kept running into the ICU, saying, "Hey Doggy, so and so has such and such."

Only Doggy knew his patients. Sick as he was, he was still practicing medicine. And then came the decline in surgery. The surgeons had not fully realized it before, but now they understood that half their surgical practice came from Doggy. Suddenly patients, even those scheduled for routine surgery, found excuses to postpone it. "I'd just as soon wait till Doggy gits back" was the standard statement. They knew Doggy wasn't going to do the surgery or even assist. They just wanted to know he was around. After a week, Hawkeye decided to let recalcitrant surgical candidates have a few words with their hero, lest the surgical world come to a standstill.

The day that Dr. Moore was released from the intensive-care unit and transferred to a private room was of historical interest. His wife Emma knew of the transfer. So, somehow, did Bette Bang-Bang, Mattress Mary and Made Marion. They were waiting in the corridor with two boxes of candy and a pot of yellow chrysanthemums.

Sixteen days after the accident, Lew the Jew Pierce and Coot Yeaton, under the cover of darkness, landed at Wooden Leg's wharf, carrying a quart of Old Bantam whiskey. Stealthily, they entered the hospital through the doctor's entrance, boarded the elevator and quietly, casually, sauntered down the hallway. They didn't bother to knock, but they opened the door of Dr. Moore's room quietly and tiptoed in.

"Hey, Doggy," said Lew, "how you feel?"

"We is some sorry, Doggy," said Coot.

"You oughta be," said Doggy.

"We brung a jug," said Lew.

"In that case," stated the physician, "all is forgiven. I'll ring for ice."

At noontime the next day Dr. Doggy Moore, despite his involvement with the jug brought by Coot and Lew the Jew, was awake, alert and ready to go.

"I'm leavin'," he announced to the head nurse.

"You can't leave unless Dr. Pierce says so, Doggy," he was told.

"Now you listen to me," said Doggy. "You go git Hawkeye and Trapper and Spearchucker and Duke and you git 'em all here. I want to talk to them."

There was a noon meeting which ended at one o'clock. The surgeons, summoned to Dr. Moore's room, arrived at 1:05 P.M.

"I'm leavin'," said Doggy. "Got somethin' to say. Three years ago, this had happened, I'd have died of a hole in my heart, but Trapper got me through that, so

I could live to have a stroke. Then Spearchucker did that endarterectomy, or whatever you call it, so I ain't paralyzed, which I would have been three years ago. Then Duke saved enough of my kidney to keep me going. By Jesus, I'm some glad I got shot in Spruce Harbor."

"Get out of here, Doggy," said Hawkeye Pierce, "and hustle up some surgery. We can't live on praise."